Chronicles of Bulinnärm

By

L Frank Turovich

A collection of epic fantasy stories set in the world of Bulinnärm. Ranging over 1000 years of history they include the first adventure of a legendary hero, the humble beginning of the greatest sorcerer who ever lived, a prince without a kingdom, and a worried librarian.

Copyright

First e-book edition: November 2015, version 1.0
Ebook ISBN: 978-1-940246-06-2
First e-book edition: November 2015, version 1.0
Print ISBN: 978-1-940246-07-9

Portions of *Chronicles of Bulinnärm* cover are © Marcus Ranum | DeviantArt.com and © Boris Jaroscak | Dreamstime.com.

Table of Contents

A Painful Blessing   5

The Huntress   29

A Lesson in Power   59

Prince of Mules   85

The Missing Wizard   115

A Post Introduction   135

Afterword   138

Other Stories   139

Chronicles of Bulinnärm

A Painful Blessing

Foreword

If you have a world with a history thousands of years old then myths and legend play a big part in the lore, as do heroes. So Bergulf Doorishmurk was born, an inspirational combination of King Arthur, Conan, Sinbad, and Paul Bunyon. Hundreds, if not thousands of his tales permeate the cultures of Bulinnärm. In some he's a hero, a champion who can do no wrong. In others, evil incarnate and cursed by the descendants who suffered from his wrath. Some tales are real, some imagined, and some mix real world events with his name to enhance the retold stories and to gain an audience. Many of these tales are collected in the book The Chronicles of the Warrior King Skar Doorishmurk, collected by famed historian Rhasiah Amourn.

Bergulf was born a simple clansman of the Worldheart Mountains, almost 2000 years after the events described as the Great Burning, when the Mythian Forest was destroyed. He was a warrior, a ship's captain, an adventurer, a king, and a hero for the ages. His tales have been told and retold and held up as examples of courage, fortitude, and sheer determination in overcoming adversity no matter what form it assumes. The following begins the saga of the legendary Skar Doorishmurk.

The howling urged Bergulf to continue running.

The youth maintained a steady relentless pace that ate up the distance even as his pursuers sought to run him down. For the last day and a night he had successfully evaded the Veritoori knights efforts to capture him. The knights sought to eradicate his residual threat to their domain, the soldiers wanted vengeance for slain comrades, and the hounds hunted for the pure joy of the kill.

Tall, rangy, with wide shoulders and strong legs, Bergulf ran on, his mountain sewn and stained leather jerkin and trousers dark with sweat, a great sword strapped tight to his back, and worn boots he had stolen from a villager that no longer needed them. Born into one of the mountain clans of Worldheart, his people were famous for their strength, endurance, fighting ability, and feared by all the lowland kingdoms. A factor the clans used every spring to raid and terrorize the lowland kingdoms.

The area he ran through now was a collection of high grasses and flowing plants, small copses of trees budding in the early spring warmth, and small hills that he used to avoid being seen while fleeing as fast as possible. He leaped over a fallen trunk right into a swarm of insects and spent the next few steps sputtering them out of his mouth. A herd of deer startled up as he jogged past, and then bounded away in fright.

His first instinct had been to fight, but soon realized he was vastly outnumbered and fled. Behind him were several Veritoori knights on horse, a bevy of soldiers on foot, and several trained hounds and handlers, all thirsting for revenge of their slain countrymen.

Bergulf continued running east.

East was home, where his clan lived, where the tribes of Worldheart survived in the highland mountains. To the North was the Oolinor forest, home of the forest *Alfr*, a reclusive race that killed trespassers on sight.

His slain raid leader Haarewalden had avoided that solemn forest as they advanced stealthily into the lowlands. That night he warned all the first time raiders of the danger. "You want to meet the gods early," said Haarewalden, "just step in there."

Warm ale had been flowing that night, a common event whenever clansmen camped. Bergulf had glanced at the tangled trees, their leaves rustling in the light breeze, but saw nothing threatening about them. Nevertheless, whether it was a true warning or just ale talking, he had no intention of ever entering.

Right now, he was backtracking along the hidden trails his clansmen had used to enter the lowlands. He knew there was a trading road somewhere to the South, but it would have made it too easy to catch him. Beyond that road lay huge bogs where savage tribes lived in a muddy delta and eked out a miserable existence among the poisonous flora that grew everywhere. The mud tribes were known to be poorer than winter ghosts, making the lowland kingdoms the prime destination for raiding.

Bergulf had hoped the rougher terrain would slow, confuse, or even lose his pursuers, but so far it had not worked. He ran on.

His breathing felt labored now, his legs aching from constant motion, and runnels of sweat soaked his torso. He was skirting a stand of trees where the dappled sunlight provided a bit of respite from the sun.

There was the sudden pounding of hooves and a Veritoori knight in red and white colors burst from the undergrowth with his axe raised. Bergulf stumbled a step then threw himself aside as it swished past his ear. That misstep made it impossible to avoid the mounts powerful shoulder that threw him loosely rolling across the ground.

Bergulf grimaced as he scrambled up, his bruised shoulder hindering his normally smooth draw. It would ache for days if he survived. He spat out dirt and set himself, his two-handed great sword ready. Blood thundered in his ears and his vision narrowed until all he saw was enemy. With an excited shout, the knight twisted his mount around, dug heels in and charged in a flurry of dirt and torn grass.

Bergulf didn't have much time. Every moment he fought meant other pursuers were drawing near. He concentrated on his opponent and waited. The rider rode to his left, then cut back at the last moment, leaned over and swung his axe at Bergulf's head.

Bergulf surged into action as he slid the knight's next swing aside with the edge of his sword. It screeched along the axe handle, and then sprung off to slice into the rider's leg. Bergulf leaned into the resistance and rode the blade as it dug into the horse's belly, leaving a gash that stretched from ribs to thigh. The knight grunted and his mount whinnied a high-pitched protest. They were by him in a second and Bergulf spun. Their second turn was slower, the horse favoring its wounded leg. Before they could recover, Bergulf was on them.

He covered the distance in three steps and swung, an upward strike that cut reins and slashed deeply into the horse's sweat and dust covered throat. Screaming, it reared and then toppled over carrying its armored rider with it. Bergulf heard equine ribs crack, followed by the distinct hollow breaking of a leg or hip. The knight's furious cries changed to an undulating scream as the writhing beast kicked and heaved its last moments atop him.

Bergulf circled, keeping well back from those deadly spasms. The knight was pinned beneath the dying horseflesh and making a futile effort to escape. When Bergulf stepped into view he stretched desperately to recover his out of reach axe, but then stopped. His helmet had fallen loose and Bergulf saw a young man barely older than himself. A new knight who had shown promise as an esquire, been promoted and trained for years and who finally earned his knighthood. His opponent raised an imploring arm, eyes wide with dread.

Bergulf stepped forward and struck so hard his sword buried itself deeply into the grass underneath. A glassy eyed head rolled away.

Blood soaked into the ground as Bergulf slumped to one knee quivering in relief, catching his breath. The adrenaline pounding in his head quieted while the blackness at the edges of his vision faded. He gingerly rotated his bruised shoulder finding it stiff but usable. He felt a thousand years old at that moment.

A howl shook off his fatigue. It sounded odd, although he could not identify why. Then he stood in understanding, the howl was from the East! The pack was now ahead of him and his escape route cut off.

Quickly he wiped the blood from his sword, sheathed it and started running, this time north.

Bergulf cursed his ill luck.

His mountain gods must surely be laughing at him now. Grim, uncompromising, and without mercy, they would view this as a test of the young clansman, a way to prove his dedication to their unyielding standards. He only had to survive.

The fight had allowed the low landers to catch up. He heard them now, crashing through the underbrush, shouts of anticipation from the soldiers, excited oaths, and encouragement from the knights and the joyful baying of the pack. They knew he was tiring. Now they were closing in for the kill.

He gritted his teeth and ran. It was all he could do. His limbs quivered as he drove them harder than before, using every trick he knew to regain lost ground. He was tiring now, and making mistakes, stumbling over roots and brush he should have easily avoided. He was leaving a trail a child could follow. His skin itched with sweaty grit, his bruised shoulder ached, and his legs trembled with exhaustion.

Ahead was the overgrowth that marked the forest edge. Behind it loomed the tall twisted trunks, gnarled branches, and heavy leaves and vegetation of the Oolinor forest.

If the gods willed, then he had one chance to escape. Enter the forest edge and wait to see what his pursuers would do. Knowing the forest's deadly reputation as they did, would they be foolish enough to enter? Bergulf was betting they would not. If so, he hoped to use their delay to slip away and escape.

Cries arose behind as his pursuers spotted him. A baying frenzy let him know that the hounds were free. Bergulf urged his trembling limbs to greater speed knowing that only the verdure woods ahead offered escape.

The panting sounds close behind sent him plunging into the arboreal darkness. The warm sunlight dimmed within steps and Bergulf found himself crashing through a maze of gnarled roots, thick hindering brush, and fallen limbs. The only illumination came from occasional shafts of light that pierced the thick canopy overhead. The boles of oak and pine surrounded him, reducing his vision to mere yards. Only steps into the *Oolinor* and already he hated the sense of brooding and suspicion it invoked. His enemies could approach and attack before he could sense them.

Without a backward glance, he plunged deeper into the forest.

He searched for a trail but saw only a jumbled, fallen mass of tree trunks, limbs, broken stumps, and other debris that reminded him more of a battlefield than a forest. The distant sound of crashing water seeped into his attention. He might have a chance if he could make that river. A flash of movement reminded him he was not safe yet.

Two large hounds were closing fast. Large, burly beasts, their tan and black bodies were barely visible in the dim forest gloom. The flash of fang and tongue were unmistakable though, as was the small growls of anticipation that rumbled from their thick throats.

There! A slope rose just to his left. He heaved forward. A little height to slow down his pursuers, making it harder to approach and provide some minor advantage. The trees thinned as the incline grew steeper and soon the youth was clawing his way up rocky slope on hands and feet. Loose rock and shale cascaded into the muzzles of two snarling hounds as they closed on him.

Bergulf threw a rock at one. It struck one hound sending it down the slope with a yelp. The second one scrambled forward and chomped at him with its wide maw. He jerked his foot away but was too slow and it caught his boot. The hound bit down and Bergulf screamed as foot bones ground together, only his heavy boot resisting the pressure. The sudden weight almost flung him from the rock face.

The hound shut its eyes, clamped its jaws tightly, and struggled to find a better foothold. Trained to hold its prey until its master arrived, it would never release him. The other hound was already scrambling back up the rocky slope. Somewhere below he heard the excited shouts of handlers. They knew he was caught.

He jammed a fist into a cleft while bracing his other foot on what he hoped was firm rock. If either slipped before he killed the hound then the mountain gods would have a good laugh at his expense. His great sword was not an option. He drew his hunting knife.

The wide blade came free with the whisper of metal scraping leather. He leaned over to slash but found his leg fully extended by the heavy animal and out of reach. It continued to worry at his boot and the pressure on grinding bones threatened to overwhelm him.

Grimacing, Bergulf strained to pull his leg upward, using every ounce of will to force weary muscles to obey. Slowly it drew upward, the hound growling defiance as it was pulled upward. Stomach and thigh muscles quivered as slowly the beast came closer.

His first slash split the beast's nostrils in a jagged line. A yelp of pain replaced the growling. Caught by instincts, the hound hung on with even more determination. Reversing his swing, Bergulf stabbed the hunting blade deep into an ear canal. A high-pitched whine replaced the yelp. His foot sent spasms up his calf. He felt knuckles scraping as his fist slipped against the gritty stone.

Bergulf felt himself weakening, his exhausted muscles unable to hold much longer. He twisted the blade savagely, until the ear was a bloody smear and the hound tumbled down the steep slope barely missing the second hound as it clambered upward.

For a second, Bergulf was sure he would follow it, his knuckles scraped raw, his foot in agony and leg shaking in spasms at its sudden release. He hung for a moment trying to remember what he had been doing. The run, the fights, the steep climb, his thoughts were a swirl of distractions.

An arrow bounced off a nearby rock. Visible through the trees below stood an archer drawing another.

"*Dromor's* balls!"

Bergulf heaved himself upward, gripping, clawing, and crawling until he rolled over the edge and out of sight. He laid gasping, bits of clear sky visible through the lighter canopy overhead. Blood flowed back into his damaged foot bringing new pain that pulsed with every heartbeat. He released the death grip on his knife; amazed it was still with him.

The roar of water sounded close now. He rolled over, and then lurched back hurriedly in shock. He was looking at a fast flowing river some eight-man lengths below him. He lay on a ridge above a narrow gorge split by a boulder-strewn river of swirling water.

He was trapped.

The slope he had once thought salvation had betrayed him. Instead of a superior position to make a stand, he had nowhere to go.

Paws scrambled for purchase behind him.

Bergulf threw himself sideways. He caught loose neck fur in a death grip before the second hound could clamp fangs into his face. Grimacing, he forced the stinking breath and drooling jaws away. Hot yellow eyes glared back malevolently while Bergulf clung to the hound's fur like a tick. If it shook him loose, could clamp those jaws on him, he was dead.

He snarled his reply and began stabbing as fast as he could. If he were to die, he would not go alone. The beast flung itself wildly from side to side, but whether to shake him loose or escape the sharp blade he could not tell. The pair struggled across the rocky ridge like weary brawlers, each move coming slower.

Bergulf fought, but knew he was weakening. His strikes were slower and the snapping fangs edged closer as the hound strained to tear and maul him. His knee slipped on a patch of loose dirt and he heard the roar of the river crashing over boulders far below. He redoubled his efforts.

A third hound clawed itself onto the ridge. It let out an excited yip as it scrambled to join the fight. Raucous shouts urging it on bellowed from below the ridgeline. The excited hound barreled into the battling pair, tumbling them all over the edge.

The fall was mercifully short and ended in a brutal splash.

Bergulf landed on the second hound in the bitterly cold water. The collision knocked the air from his lungs and he felt a rib crack. The rushing water carried them down into turbulent depths. He pushed the limp bleeding body away and tried to locate the surface but could see nothing. The current dragged him along the bottom and he was helpless to resist. His bitten foot slammed against an unseen object. He screamed and felt the icy water rush into mouth and nose.

With flailing arms and legs, he fought his way through the chaotic pull of currents. The weight of his great sword was slowing and dragging him down against his every effort. Bergulf knew if he did not find the surface soon it would not matter.

The intense cold burned his body, numbed his hands, slowed his reactions, and dulled control of his bruised and exhausted form. He slapped against a lichen slick boulder. Desperate, he fought to hold on, but it slipped away. Another bruising encounter, this time clawing fingers found a notch to halt his uncontrolled plunge down the river. With his last bit of strength he hung on, then surged upward until his head exploded out of the water and he inhaled deeply. Air had never tasted so sweet.

He lay for an endless time choking out water and recovering while the river threatened to tear him from the safety of his perch.

A stiff body slammed against him, almost tearing him loose and he watched the dead hound drift away. Behind it, the head of the third hound fought the current, its focus entirely on him, wide toothy jaws open in savage anticipation.

Bergulf clung tighter to the slippery rock. He could not defend himself. His hunting knife was gone and he dared not grab at his sword or the river would send him tumbling down the rapids again.

The hound fought closer until it was barely a man length away. Bergulf saw grim determination in that burning gaze and tensed himself in readiness. Without warning, the fierce head dipped below the turbulent water. Bergulf searched desperately to spot the creature.

Angry shouts caused him to look up.

Several soldiers, some in the red and white colors of Veritoori shook weapons and cursed him. A couple drew arrows and aimed. Fully exposed on the slick rock and with no means to resist, Bergulf did the only thing he could and let go.

The roiling current swept him away in its powerful grip.

Bergulf awoke with a groan.

It was difficult to breathe and his entire body throbbed in pain. He lay for a moment and took stock of his condition. Rough pebbles poked into his bruised body while cold water lapped over feet. Bruises, both old and new made every bit of creaky movement awkward. He forced open a swollen eye, and clamped it shut at the shocking brightness. He tried again, this time slowly and let it adjust. Instead of a forest canopy overhead there was clear sky with a few tree limbs sticking into his view from somewhere above where his head lay. His gaze rotated down and stopped.

A sword blade rested against his throat.

Cautiously his eye traveled up the blade toward its owner, a slim figure in garments colored like the forest, from gray to multiple shades of forest leaves. Almond shaped, leaf green eyes glowered at him from above a concealing veil. *Alfr* eyes!

A tendril of fear slid down his spine. The *Alfr* were an ancient race that had once battled giants to control the world, but then lost it with the arrival of *Dwarvulk* clans and humans. They now lived exclusively in the major forests of Bulinnärm, avoiding all contact with the lesser races and killing any that entered their wooded refuges. And he was in their domain now.

"Don't move," said the *Alfr*.

Bergulf glared, furious at being caught. He ignored the sword resting on his throat, its owner's stern demeanor, and his weakened state. A Worldheart clansman did not die like this, an animal. He would not lie waiting to be slaughtered. He shifted slightly; preparing muscles and will for one last act of defiance.

The figure shifted and there was blackness again.

"You're awake," spoke a voice.

He lay on his side, hands and feet bound tightly, his body a mass of bruises, one foot still numb. An odd smell mixed with the smoke and warmth of a nearby fire. In the flickering light he saw bandages and realized the smell must come from the medicinal herbs used to bind his wounds. He strained covertly at his bounds, testing for weakness, but found none.

Bergulf forced himself up. Eventually he wiggled into a sitting position facing his captor. The dancing flames and drab clothing merged seamlessly, making it difficult to separate the slight figure from the background. A pale face with ruddy highlights hovered motionless in the darkness.

The hooded face was narrow, almost pinched, with large solemn eyes that gazed at him without emotion. The cloaked figure appeared unconcerned at Bergulf's examination, quietly sitting with hands resting on knees. A tall bow rested within reach while a sword hilt peeked from beneath a cloak. Bergulf's own great sword and clothes were piled nearby.

Bergulf licked chapped lips. "Water?"

A small waterskin arced through the flames and landed near his feet. It took considerable effort to twist his bound body close enough to grab the waterskin. He pulled the plug loose with his teeth and nearly dropped the precious contents in his haste. With some additional contortions he was finally able to drink. He did greedily, portions slopping down chin and throat before landing on his groin. He emptied it in a single long draw that left him sated yet wanting more.

He shook the empty waterskin at his captor. "Thanks."

The face grimaced slightly, so fast Bergulf thought maybe it was just a shadow of flickering fire light.

They camped beneath an earthen berm of exposed rocks and clay while knotted roots jutted around them like arms ready to embrace. The grassy area upon which they sat ended just inside the fire's glow before changing into water smooth pebbles and flood debris. Somewhere beyond that he heard the burble of a water, probably the river he had fallen into. He glanced at his captor and was sure. Someone that size would not have been able to drag him too far.

"Why?"

The soprano voice was a whisper over the sounds of river and crackling fire. It sounded curious and yet carried no emotion.

"You appear to have your wits, yet you enter."

"Not my choice," said Bergulf.

"Choice? You choose death over what awaited you outside?"

Bergulf spat. "The Veritoori have their ways."

He shuddered at the thought. The Veritoori's lust for vengeance against a captured clansman was not something raiders considered. Those tales had also been shared during winter. The most terrifying ones involved their women who relished a chance to humiliate and flay the killers of their husbands, brothers, fathers, sons, and other kin. Bergulf shuddered at the memories.

"You are young." The slim face tilted. "The young never fear death. It is not a concept they understand, nor seek to learn." Emerald eyes bore into his. "How old are you?"

"Old enough to raid," said Bergulf. "I have seen ten and six summers."

"So young." The green eyes closed, then opened and gazed at him sadly. "The law allows no choice in this. Now you will never learn."

"Law? What law?"

"The law states you must face the challenge for entering the sacred forest. Only *Alfr* may tread its blessed grounds safely, *Dwarvulk* and humans are forbidden."

"Just let me go. Cut me loose and I'll leave. I'll never return."

"I will know, and so will *Noaa*."

"*Noaa?*"

"The Spirit of the *Oolinor*, the guardian of my people, the living god who watches over and protects this realm from intruders. Like you."

"I'm no danger to you or your god, even if I wasn't hurt. I was trying to return home, forced to enter here by men pursuing me. I'll leave." He extended bound hands as far as he could and allowed a pleading tone to enter his voice. "Cut me loose and I'll never return. By *Dromor*, I swear."

The *Alfr* sat quietly, face turned away in thought while Bergulf waited patiently. Had he been too earnest? He knew he could overpower the slim alfr even in his weakened condition. He would take whatever supplies the alfr carried and leave this damned forest. It was a surprise really. From stories he had thought them more dangerous, not weak, as this one was.

Somewhere far off a faint animal roar echoed through the still trees, a night hunter celebrating its kill. The *Alfr* sat up rigidly, then shook its head and looked at him. Bergulf saw a renewed sense of conviction on the slim face.

"No," said the alfr. "You are young, yet lie like a veteran."

Bergulf raged. He strained, throwing all his strength into pulling his wrists apart in a massive effort to burst the bindings that held him. He fell over surging and pulling until exhaustion ended his effort. Sweat dripped from forehead and torso. Across the fire the *Alfr* stood, bow held in position, ready to draw and release at a moments notice. Even if he had broke free he would have been pierced before taking a step. He panted and let his anger drain away like rain into dry ground.

The *Alfr* lowered the bow and sat down.

"You cannot break those bonds. They can barely be cut, nor broken. What's your name?"

"Bergulf."

"A strong name, for a human. Mine is Tywynn. In my language it means *Sun Rising Brilliantly in Glorious Radiance above Dancing Morning Leaves*. What does Bergulf mean?"

"Bergulf? It's just a name."

"How sad," said Tywynn, "Names are important. They are tokens from the gods and important. I did not know human names meant so little to you. Rest now. We have far to travel tomorrow and you will need strength."

"Where are we going?"

"To my tribe, it is where your challenge will be judged."

"You'll let me die then?"

"It is a choice, but very likely." Tywynn shivered, and then threw a blanket at him. "May *Noaa* take pity on your soul."

The next morning Bergulf followed Tywynn into *Oolinor*.

The clammy clothes chafed Bergulf's skin as he struggled to keep up with the swift moving *Alfr*. The small figure ahead slipped through the rugged floor of the forest as effortlessly as a fox. Bergulf labored over the same terrain like an elderly ox. The silent figure kept constant tension on a rope lead, now wrapped around Bergulf's neck, forcing him to keep up. When not searching the ground for obstacles to avoid, Bergulf glared defiantly at Tywynn and waited.

Around mid-morning, the *Alfr* found a small stream where they stopped and refilled their empty water skins. Bergulf clumsily sat and breathed deeply as he stretched aching legs and feet. He tried to remember how many days he had been running, first to escape death and now to it. It seemed like forever.

Tywynn tossed over a filled skin, making sure to keep out of reach. "Drink, you will need it."

"How much farther?" Bergulf asked.

Before the *Alfr* could respond a baying of dogs echoed through the lush forest. Tywynn cocked an ear, and then leapt back as Bergulf hurriedly scrambled up.

"*Kara's dice!*" He looked around wildly. "Give me a weapon."

"Who is that?" Tywynn asked.

"The bastards that ran me in here, that's who."

The *Alfr* said angrily. "You bring more of your kind into this sacred place? *Noaa* will see them dead as well."

"Would that your god listens," Bergulf muttered, tugging at his bonds. "Maybe he will, but not until they kill us."

"You are concerned?"

"Look, those knights want one thing, my head. And if you're around, yours as well."

A thunderous roar interrupted the baying, immediately followed by yelps of pain and angry challenging growls. Human shouts interspersed with screams and fighting noises echoed dimly.

"*Noaa* has found them," said Tywynn. The *Alfr* turned away. "Come, let us continue."

Bergulf saw his chance and attacked.

He charged forward, fists clenched together, and swung at the *Alfr's* exposed neck as silently as he could. He hoped to knock the *Alfr* unconscious and then recover his great sword. He had considered killing the arrogant *Alfr* but knew he would only have time to grab his weapons and run. The *Alfr* would have enough to do when the Veritoori found him.

Tywynn was no longer there.

The *Alfr* slipped aside and Bergulf's blow missed. He stumbled past awkwardly. With snakelike speed and total indifference, Tywynn swung his bow. Bergulf suddenly had no control over his arms or legs as he fell to his knees, then keeled over. He must have blacked out because when he awoke there was water dribbling onto his face and a throbbing at the base of his skull. Why was he on the ground?

The *Alfr* dragged him up. The shouts of fighting and roaring sounded closer to Bergulf. "Hurry, they approach." He followed the persistent tug at his neck as fast as his legs could move. The sounds of fighting faded and Bergulf's mind cleared. He watched the *Alfr* with more respect now. He was not as weak as Bergulf had thought.

They walked for a long time. Tywynn soon lead them away from the trail and into wilder areas of undergrowth, where lightning struck stumps, and huge oak and fir trees abounded. Wild birds fell silent as they passed, watching them with unblinking eyes.

Tywynn stopped as another rumbling roar sounded from behind. It was much closer. The *Alfr* froze for a moment and Bergulf could not decide if it was in shock or fear.

"*Noaa* hunts." Tywynn tugged the rope again. "Hurry."

They burst into a clearing, a meadow filled with waving grass, light blue flowers and clouds of swarming insects. The sounds of pursuit were louder. They raced across the area and slid into the shadows just as an arrow thrummed by Bergulf's head and buried itself in a tree. Tywynn turned, pulled, and released almost before Bergulf could look back. His stomach clutched. The hasty bowman was falling over, Tywynn's arrow visible in his neck. But it was the two Veritoori knights and five soldiers that worried Bergulf. They were barely a spear throw away and approaching fast.

"Give me a weapon," Bergulf said.

Tywynn glanced at him.

"You can't fight them all. Give me a weapon."

The *Alfr* considered for so long Bergulf thought about attacking again. Without a word Tywynn slashed his bindings, and then slipped the great sword from his back before tossing it over.

Bergulf stripped the loose rope from his wrists and neck, and pulled his weapon from its scabbard. The thrill of holding it again poured new strength into his body. He swung the sword idly around, his aches and pains forgotten as he loosened his muscles for the coming battle. He was done running. He should have never started. He turned to face the Veritoori knights, sword at the ready.

Tywynn stood nearby with a pair of fine swords.

The knights drew up a dozen paces away before leading their soldiers into a semi-circle of swords, maces, and short spears around Bergulf and Tywynn. The knights once splendid armor and clothing showing evidence of hard use, grimy from dirt, stained with runnels of rust, and the stink of tired and sweaty men too long on the hunt.

"Two savages," said one of the knights, "and one an *Alfr*." He pointed his sword at Tywynn. "Capture that one, for the king."

Then he pointed at Bergulf.

"But that one," he grimaced a feral grin at Bergulf, "that one dies."

The knights and their men attacked and Bergulf was fighting for his life.

The knights concentrated on Bergulf and he quickly deflecting their initial attacks, taking note of their tactics. The talkative one was the better fighter, patient with his strikes, quick to riposte, and cunning enough to take advantage of any weakness Bergulf exposed. The other knight beat at him with a sturdy mace that threatened to tear his great sword loose and countered all of Bergulf's strikes with a colorful shield. Bergulf dodged, countered, deflected, and moved as fast as his weary legs allowed, waiting for a chance.

To his right Tywynn moved like a shade, twin swords weaving a wall of steel before him. The soldiers had been too eager to fight the *Alfr* and were now crowding each other and hindering their attacks. One reeled away with a scream as an *Alfr* blade slashed across his chest.

The moment came when a mountain of russet fur shambled out of the shadows and into the Veritoori. Gaping black jaws filled with fangs enveloped the bleeding man. Before he could scream the beast snapped jaws shut, threw its massive head back and a headless body spiraled away. It happened so fast the remaining knights and fighters barely registered their companion's death. Then it was among them. Two more soldiers died in screams as black and curved claws as long as Bergulf's fingers ripped one asunder and stove in a second chest.

"*Noaa!*"

Bergulf gaped at Tywynn. Shit, his god was a druin!

On four legs, it was as tall as he was, with a head like a barrel, a burly neck bristling with stiffened fur raised in waves along the shoulders and back. It reminded Bergulf of a bear, yet one sized to make even the gods tremble. Buried beneath jutting brow ridges, Bergulf saw intelligence in those round black eyes, not the furious rage of a beast, but a calculating cunning that made his blood run cold.

The druin roared defiance as the Veritoori knights faced this new terror. The ground vibrated and small limbs and leaves fell from nearby trees. Bergulf could feel the beast's anger reverberate through his bones, and he longed to be anywhere else. The druin stood on its hind paws, a solid wall of hairy threat.

"To me, rally to me," screamed the tall knight on recognizing the greater danger. The fighters around Tywynn disengaged to join their leader. The second knight scowled at Bergulf before stepping back and rushing to join the men now encircled around the towering beast. The druin roared again and just for a second its opponents shrunk back, and then on command they attacked as one.

Bergulf was right there with them.

The second knight swung his mace but was knocked away by a pawed backhand that splintered his shield into kindling. The remaining fighters attacked from the side, but one was disemboweled for moving too slow, the other stepped away with a look of panic, turned and ran, leaving the tall knight and Bergulf facing the enraged druin.

The Veritoori knight fought superbly, his blade weaving a bloody trail across the limbs, chest, and belly of the looming beast. Bergulf assisted with savage swings that chopped off hunks of bloody fur and muscle. For all the damage the two warriors were doing, the beast was not slowing. Every swing was fast and unstoppable, and a clean strike from one of those huge paws would end the fight.

Sweat dripped into Bergulf's eyes as he avoided another clawing strike. His return blow left a ragged slash along the already red-striped and dripping limb. He whispered to his gods for strength and wondered if they could hear him this deep in this *Alfr* forest.

The druin shifted from defense to offense in an instant, collapsing down and over the knight with a black maw open wide exposing the long yellow fangs within. There was a smothered cry of surprise and then a shuddering scream as those fangs crunched into a Veritoori skull before blessed silence.

Bergulf backed away. His chest heaved and arms trembled from exhaustion. It was now a one-on-one fight and the druin held all the advantages.

The druin spat out the crushed skull and let the loose body fall before shifting awkwardly to face Bergulf. In those coal black eyes was reflected his death. The beast drew closer, blood dripping from numerous wounds. Bergulf cursed and prepared himself to die, when an arrow sprouted in the druin's cheek.

Tywynn had stood aside during the entire battle, making no effort to assist in killing the druin. The beast spun its baleful glare of hatred on the *Alfr* and stiffly changed direction. Tywynn seemed rooted in place, his empty bow held in limp fingers, seemingly frozen immobile by the approach of his living god.

Bergulf raised his two-handed sword and charged forward roaring, "Run!"

The druin roared and swung. Tywynn shook off his lethargy but had waited too long. The wheel sized paw knocked the small figure away like a child's doll.

Bergulf saw a chance and struck. The beast shifted and his sword buried itself between ribs and shoulder bone and not the neck as he had intended. He drove it using all the force of his rush and remaining strength to bury it deep. The druin flayed back and only his closeness to the musky chest saved him from the full power of its initial blow. He staggered away empty handed and caught the return of yellow claws that slashed into cheek and head. The blinding strike rolled him across the blood-strewn field until an unmoving body stopped him.

Blood dripped down his face like hot rain. The claws had just missed his left eye, ripping three grooves into skin that arced from mouth, across cheek and eye, and ending somewhere in his hairline. The rents would take forever to heal, if he survived. He tried to stand but his boots slid away and he fell back. The druin lumbered closer, the open jaws and blood stained fangs dominating his vision.

"*Noaa!*"

The druin spun around like a creature half its size. Another *Alfr* arrow protruded from a haunch. The druin bit at the fletching and tore part of the arrow away. With an angry growl it looked for its tormentor. Several steps away stood Tywynn, battered and begrimed, standing awkwardly on one leg as he aimed another arrow.

Bergulf staggered up and swayed. He searched the ground for a weapon, any weapon. There, the Veritoori knight's sword lay half under the man's body. He stumbled forward and tugged weakly at the blade. Finally, it was in his hands, he turned to see the druin charge and batter Tywynn aside like a child. The alfr slammed against a tree and lay unmoving.

His body screamed as he forced himself forward. He held the blade low and aimed for the druin's neck again. He raced at the shaggy body. With a final surge, he buried the point as deep into the neck as he could. The fur smelled of musk and wildness, of green grass, and blood as the druin roared in agony. It convulsed and Bergulf was thrown aside. He rolled to a stop and tried to stand, but had no strength and collapsed. His sword was lost, or it was still in the beast. He could no longer remember. There was a thrashing behind him, a roar that seemed to go on forever, and then darkness.

Bergulf felt gentle fingers touching his face. It was Tywynn wrapping a poultice around the raw claw marks that striped cheek and forehead. The *Alfr's* face was swollen and bruised in a colorful mosaic that did little to conceal a flat expression. Bergulf's mouth was as dry as desert sand and he felt light headed. He licked his lips, wincing when the action pulled at his wounds.

"Here," said Tywynn. The *Alfr* tilted a waterskin into Bergulf's lips and he reveled as the cool, slightly leathery tasting water poured into him. He had never tasted anything so refreshing. When finished, he examined the *Alfr* closely, noting tightness around the lips he had not seen before.

"The druin…"

"Dead, it shall bother us no more."

He shifted arms and legs to determine if he had any additional injuries. Stiff limbs protested but nothing seemed to be broken or missing. It was a good fight if all you walked away with were scars and wounds that would heal. No serious damage, other than the facial wound. Tywynn looked battered as well, and Bergulf sensed the reluctant *Alfr* had more to say. Finally, he asked, "You okay?"

Tywynn's face frowned as he considered a response.

"You survived." Tywynn spoke in a whisper.

A strong herbal smell floated from the poultice. Bergulf touched the bandage carefully.

"You will have majestic scars." Tywynn inhaled deeply before speaking again. "Your descendants will sing of this day."

"Descendants?"

Tywynn looked down and away. "You have proven yourself worthy of the challenge, and by law, you are free."

Bergulf shook his head. Free? "You mean…"

The *Alfr* pointed at Bergulf's sword. "Take your weapon and go." The *alfr* turned away but looked troubled.

Bergulf slowly stood, every movement a painful reminder. Was this a trick? He seized the familiar hilt of his great sword. It needed some sharpening but that could wait. He wiped it clean, and then sheathed it. "Why the change? You wanted me to die before."

Tywynn spun to face him. "No, it is simply what normally happens. Only one other has ever survived *Noaa's* challenge."

"*Noaa*? That thing was *Noaa*?"

"No, the druin was but a vessel for *Noaa*. Even now he resides in another, watching and protecting us, waiting for the next challenger to appear." Tywynn chewed a cheek. "He has not been defeated for hundreds of years. The last time…" The voice trailed off. "It was long ago."

Bergulf thought he understood. To defeat a living god, even if it lived in a druin, must be quite an achievement. It would make for a great tale around the winter fires someday.

Tywynn was examining his face. "*Noaa* has favored you."

"What?"

"That wound, it will scar well. You were touched by a god and survived. You have gained great honor among the *Alfr* for that. The scar proves you are strong, fearless, and a dangerous warrior. *Noaa* favors those with a token of his respect. It will strike fear into your enemies."

Bergulf looked at the *Alfr* in disbelief. Battle scars definitely marked warriors of fighting ability and fierceness in battle. He grimaced painfully.

"I will call you Skar," said Tywynn.

Skar?

"It means *Righteous Challenger of the Gods*, but humans translate it to be *Godslayer*."

Bergulf considered. It was simple, direct, the very name of a mighty warrior, unlike his birth name. He rolled it around on his tongue, tasting its form, feeling its weight and inherent power.

Yes, Skar Doorishmurk. It was a good name.

The Huntress

Foreword

One of my main storylines revolves around a man named Hieronymus who has been cursed with magical abilities. On Bulinnärm there is immense distrust of magic ever since an Alfr sorcerer destroyed the vast Mythian Forest and created the modern Urdraxion Desert, a vast wasteland of blasted rock, blowing sand and hostile creatures. The story that follows introduces Hieronymus as he first learns he has magic and the ramifications of that knowledge.

"There's strangers here," said Kaevan.

Hieronymus stretched and let his fingers rub at the dull ache in his forehead after another long day of working the nets with his father was over. Around him the dozen boats that made up the tiny fishing fleet of Braewickinn finished transferring the days catch into wooden tubs for transport. Men and boys he had known his whole life laughed and joked as they tied down their boats and headed home well before dusk. It was a special day, for tonight they celebrated the Festival of Aellissea.

He was excited too, the festival was an annual event celebrating the arrival of spring, the blossoming of the land, and the blessing of the sea. It was a night of food, drink, and dancing in the warm open air after a winter of cramped living. A night that cast off the pall of winter and promised a new year of joy and abundance. He smiled in eager anticipation, for Fulimera would be there as well.

"There's always strangers in town."

Kaevan looked like a melon ready to burst. His face was flush, his eyes wide, his lips pursed as he fought to restrain himself. They had known each other since they were toddlers, so Hieronymus was used to seeing his friend bursting with secrets to share. Kaevan seemed constitutionally unable to hold anything back and was forever blurting things out. His openness played well against Hieronymus' more hesitant and careful nature.

"Not like these," said Kaevan. "They're different."

Hieronymus stopped rubbing his temple and looked down at his friend. He tried to recall a time when he didn't tower over everyone. He now stood over a head higher than every one of his neighbors as well as every stranger he had ever seen. He swallowed an angry comment. He had to watch himself when his head throbbed. It was too easy to lose control and scream, to lash out at those closest to him in frustration and anger, even his best friend.

Kaevan blinked rapidly, then the torrent of words began.

"There's three of them, two men and a woman," Kaevan blurted out. "The men look like fighters, with swords and armor. Not new either. Looks like they've seen a battle or two." His face squinted in thought. "They could be guards, but that woman, she doesn't need them. She doesn't dress like a woman, what with breeches and jerkin instead of a dress." Kaevan looked around warily. "She looks fancy, but she's got a face that reminds me of Peaver's old tom. Mean eyed and spoiling for a fight if you ask me."

His friend was a typical Braewickinn villager, sporting a compact frame, with wide shoulders, strong arms, and an infectious spirit that could never be quenched for long. After all these years, Hieronymus still wondered how Kaevan managed to remain so open and optimistic, especially under the current situation.

Both would soon be considered adults and the village elders frowned upon almost adults not helping, so they were put to work.

Kaevan worked as a cooper with his father, spending every day cutting, sanding, and forming wood boards into staves and then steaming them into proper form to become stout fish barrels. Hieronymus spent his days throwing nets off the back of his father's small fishing vessel and then hauling in loads of rill-rill, a delicacy outside of the village, which were then dutifully packed into the new barrels. When enough were filled to capacity, they were transported to nearby towns and sold for badly needed silver. It was important yet dull work, and not exactly the life either of them had dreamed of when children.

"Who asked you?" Hieronymus poked at Kaevan to distract him.

"Stop that." Kaevan slapped away the poking finger. "You did. You stopped right here and asked me to tell you."

Hieronymus shook his head slowly and smiled.

"That's it? You saw a couple of fighters and a mean woman? That's your news?"

"You'll see. Wait until tonight. You won't miss them."

Hieronymus flayed wildly with upraised hands. "Of course I'll see them, we know everyone in Braewickinn, strangers stand out like fishing lamps across an open sea." He placed a hand on Kaevan's shoulder. "Did they say anything? What about the war at Worldheart?"

Kaevan shook off the hand. "Nothing." He kicked a loose stone fiercely. "Not like it makes a difference to us."

Hieronymus slapped Kaevan's back in camaraderie. His friend was right. What chance did they have to leave? They had been born into a tiny fishing village and a simple if hard life. They would raise families devoted to making ends meet, and spend the rest of their lives working to support themselves until they passed that toil onto their own sons and daughters. The boys bonded when they discovered a mutual desire to escape their dull existence, that of being anywhere but Braewickinn, preferably doing something exciting.

The occasional traveler brought new stories that enthralled the youngsters. It didn't matter how insignificant or old the stories were, just hearing about faraway places made village life seem less dull. Hieronymus longed to visit some of the great cities he'd learned of from books and traveler tales; the busy seaport of Duerlorn, the twin kingdoms of Kyr-Ansar and Kyr-Darst, and oh, to see the majestic walls of the emperor's capital, mighty Alexiandrölarn itself.

Somehow he knew it would never came to pass. Both had been dragged protesting into the respective family businesses and their dreams ground away like wheat under a mill wheel. New travelers meant a chance for news, and it sounded like Hieronymus would have to get it himself.

He slapped his sullen friend's back and took off running. He yelled back, "Come on, I'll race you."

"Cheater!"

Hieronymus beat Kaevan to town easily, the lope of his long legs far exceeding that of his smaller friend. Gasping a bit from the run they went their separate ways.

"Don't take long," said Kaevan.

"Stop worrying, I'll be there."

Hieronymus just had time to wipe the smell of rill-rill from his body and change into his best clothes, his only unpatched trousers too short by far and a flowing shirt colored like the sea and reaching mid-thigh. He ran fingers through his wavy hair badly in need of a trim. Unhappy with the results he wrapped a leather tie around it and let it project a small tuft down his neck.

"Stay out of trouble," said his mother. She pecked nattily at his clothes, pulling here, patting there while Hieronymus waited patiently. His mother, a tiny bustle of energy looked him over carefully. As the village's main seamstress, she was always over concerned and spending too much time worrying about his appearance. Many of the dresses and holiday clothes he would see tonight had come by way of her nimble and busy fingers.

She patted his cheek. "You tell Fuli hello," she said with a smile.

"Mom!"

At Hieronymus' intense blush, her eyes twinkled in merriment. "From me, from me, of course. We've talked and your father agrees, you're too young. Another year and you'll be ready."

"Mom! I like Fuli, but I can't settle down. I want to travel first, see some of the kingdoms."

"You travel all the time," said his mother. "With your father to Brularn."

"That's not traveling mom, that's hauling fish to market. I want to see a real city, a big one, like Choy or Alexiandrölarn."

His mother puckered her lips. Born and raised in Braewickiɔn she had lived her entire life within its boundaries, finally marrying and settled into raising a family. After five children, she turned to sewing in her home to earn extra obols. The quality of her work soon led to a constant stream of orders that helped supplement the family's income. Letting her husband occasionally travel to the nearest market was necessary, but to pack up and move someplace else, oh no, she was having none of that.

"Your a good boy Hieronymus, but its time to accept life as it is. Your life is here, in Braewickinn, not traipsing all over the country and getting into trouble." He winced as she patted his cheek again. His mother's tone changed to concern.

"Headache again, do you need some berrybrook tea?"

"Mom, I'm fine."

"Your sure?"

He grabbed her tiny hands and did his best reassuring smile. "I'm fine mom, stop worrying."

"But I do," his mother said softly.

"Kaevan's waiting, Mom, I've got to go."

Hieronymus hurried outside where the cool sea breeze smelled clean and intoxicating, a distinct change from the stale fishiness of winter. It buoyed Hieronymus' attitude and before long he arrived at the swirling exuberance that was the spring festival.

It looked like everyone in the village and the surrounding households were celebrating, turning the normally quiet village center into a cacophony of music, laughter, and general merriment. The past winter was considered a mild one by the coastal village, but the dreary months of gray skies, leaden water, and stormy weather had done little to keep everyone in light spirit.

The storefronts were covered with spring flowers, sheaved together and hanging from rooftops. Colorful ribbons and woven multi-colored bunting draped doorways and windows, looped between buildings and decorated every spare cornice and rooftop. Bright ribbons of cotton and rare silk hung around the necks of celebrating villagers as people greeted one another in carefree voices. It was more activity than Hieronymus had seen in months. The scent of roasting sheep made his stomach gurgle quietly in anticipation.

When he found Fuli, what would he say?

There was Gruwl, known for his bullying ways, raising steins with the fisherman Lonnigin and Toiby, men whom he normally argued with on sight. Innkeeper Jollos sat comfortably in the back of a huge wagon from which he was dispensing his famous spring brew to red-cheeked villagers who laughed and joked together in jovial conversation. Children ran everywhere, the Hullsoomer twins screaming in merriment as they chased each other in an elaborate game of find the rill-rill as Miery, their mother, smiled on in amusement.

Hieronymus threaded his way through the loose crowd with no real destination in mind as he soaked up the excitement of his neighbors. There were the familiar faded paintings of successful harvests and fishing voyages with gods and goddess looking down hung everywhere. Innkeeper Jollos only hung them out for the festival and Hieronymus was happy to see the familiar scenes once again. In front of the meeting hall, a carved image of the goddess Aellissea stood in a lacquered shrine nearly hidden by offerings beseeching her for a successful season of fishing and harvesting.

The annual festival was always a welcome relief in Braewickinn, a familiar event that lightened hearts and raised the spirits of everyone after the winter months. The rill-rill schools would soon be swarming everywhere and for a few months the fishing, packing, and selling of the harvest would keep all of them busy.

"Happy festival Hieronymus," said a soft voice.

Hieronymus started and turned where Fulimera stood suppressing a laugh, the pounding in his chest matching that in his head.

"Uh, hi," Hieronymus stammered out, "Fuli."

Fulimera stood nearly as tall as Hieronymus, coming almost to his shoulders. She had huge eyes that gazed at him over high cheekbones framed within an oval face, her honey colored hair hanging to her waist in loose braids, held together with matching blue ribbons. She wore one of his mother's creations, slim and swirling, and colored to accent the sea blue of her eyes. Her sudden appearance left him speechless. He gaped like a beached fish, struggling to think of something to say that didn't make him sound like an idiot.

"Are you enjoying the festival?" Fulimera's eyes sparkled. Behind her like guards stood her cousins Julifene and Ambri, of similar features and hair coloring. They were her closest friends and wore more of his mother's creations, Julifene's in rose and Ambri a summer green. Julifene smirked at Hieronymus' discomfort while Ambri seemed distracted, looking at something behind him.

"Uh, sure. I mean, yes, yes I am."

"Good," said Fulimera. "Maybe I'll see you later."

Fulimera turned and glided away, Julifene and Ambri trailing in her wake and reminding him of young ducklings. Hieronymus watched them go, silently cursing his reluctant tongue, face burning with embarrassment. He rubbed at his forehead absently. His headache was back. With it a sudden memory arose.

"My mom says hello!" He winced as he blurted it out.

Fulimera glanced back at him, flashed a quick smile and turned and faded into the crowd. Hieronymus slumped nonplussed.

Why was he so stupid?

"Have you seen them?"

For the second time that night Hieronymus jumped in surprise as Kaevan's loud voice interrupted his interpretation of Fuli's mysterious glimpse.

"Stop doing that!"

Kaevan ignored Hieronymus' irritation completely.

"Come on, you got to see this."

Kaevan grabbed his arm and began guiding him through the milling crowd. The festival was certainly livening up. The celebratory colors were now dulled by the darkening night as Aellissea sank behind the dark sea and torches and lanterns gleamed everywhere, their flickering light throwing moving shadows everywhere. The people of Braewickinn thronged the main square now while a trio of musicians played a merry tune. Several couples were kicking clouds of dust with their enthusiastic dancing.

Everywhere he saw people enjoying life with their friends and neighbors, the joy of the festival and drinks loosening their normally reserved nature. Well, almost everywhere.

There was a quieter spot in the crowd, along the walkway in front of the inn. Normally that spot was filled with villagers drinking and yelling crude yet good-natured encouragements to the musicians and dancing couples below. This year it looked like the best positions had been taken over by three strangers. The locals gave them a wide berth and stood at one end while the strangers stood silently surveying the milling crowd.

There was an aura about them that screamed, keep away.

Braewickinn visitors were usually traders, tinkers, travelling shows, puppeteers, musicians, or the rare mercenary between jobs. A troop of Duerlorn cavalry once rode through the village causing no end of excitement and gossip as they spent the night and departed without stating a word of their purpose. Leaving behind a young Hieronymus the memory of their dark green uniforms emblazoned with a flying sea falcon in white. Jollos still boasted of their visit.

The trio did not look like anything Hieronymus had ever seen before, they were something else. The two hard looking men flanked the third, a slim woman nearly invisible between her larger partners. Hieronymus tugged against Kaevan's grip, slowing their advance. His headache surged and he was reluctant to get any closer.

"Come on," said Kaevan.

"I see them."

His height made it easy to look over the crowd. The odd trio stood between two bright lanterns allowing Hieronymus a good look. What he saw was intimidating. These men wore the look of killers as they examined the crowd like wolves surveying a flock of sheep, measuring each for dinner. Dressed in dark gray underneath boiled leather cuirasses that was finer than anything Hieronymus had ever seen before. No emblems adorned their clothes to indicate alliance and the shifting crowd prevented Hieronymus from seeing their weapons. Somehow he knew they had seen plenty of use.

If the men were intimidating, the woman was worse.

The tiny woman, slim, wore a haughty expression that radiated anger like an oven. If the men were wolves she was the pack leader, aloof and deadly. Unlike the men she was dressed in fine travel clothes of leather jerkin and brown trousers while a patterned cape hung from her narrow shoulders. A large silver necklace hung between her small breasts and rings encircled every finger that rested on the walkway railing. She squinted over the crowd in sullen purpose; searching for something only she could see. Her searching gaze turned and Hieronymus felt his throbbing head clang in stabbing agony.

Her gaze widened as it locked on Hieronymus.

He staggered in Kaevan's grip as intense pain stabbed into his temples. His knees felt weak and sick to his stomach. Through watering eyes he saw her point him out to one of her companions.

"That one," he heard clearly.

The wolves did not hesitate. At the woman's gesture they started forward, shoving through the crowd towards where Hieronymus and Kaevan stood. He struggled to collect his thoughts. His headaches had never been this bad before, constant, annoying, and irritating, but never debilitating. When he opened his eyes the wolves stood before him. The hairs on his neck rose and everything in his vision narrowed down to the hard emotionless faces before him.

They stood slightly apart, hands resting on worn sword hilts, alert and wary at the same time. The older, more grizzled one spoke first, his mean-eyed companion watching intently.

"Lady Ilarhia wants you."

The stabbing pains in his head continued, distracting him. If anything, they seemed to throb in time with the man's gruff tone. Hieronymus swayed, the voice coming from a vast distance, the crowd noises fading into a low background murmur, like waves of an incoming storm. He tried to concentrate and saw the lips moving, but heard nothing.

"Now!" The second man grabbed Hieronymus's arm.

Kaevan knocked the hand away. "Leave him alone."

Casually the man backhanded Kaevan, sending him sprawling along with a couple of nearby celebrants who emitted startled yelps. Kaevan bounced up; blood running down a swelling lip and rushed back, only to meet a hard fist that folded him in two. The crowd drew away from the fracas leaving Hieronymus standing dazed and alone while Kaevan gulped for air. He felt nauseous, the lanterns flaring at him, the music, voices, and crowd's laughter harsh and incredibly loud. He thought he saw warden Thorath barging through the gathering crowd as the men stepped forward. Maybe he would intervene. He was sure he saw the strange woman's lips curling in a capricious smile.

With a cold shudder his strange passivity dropped and Hieronymus realized he was in danger. He panicked.

Without a word, he turned and ran.

He charged through the ring of spectators gathered around to see the commotion and into the less crowded square. He rushed past; heedless of those he knocked aside in his determined effort to escape. He glanced behind once to see Kaevan wrestling the leg of one stranger as the other pursued.

He dodged around Ambri who stared at him with alarm, sidestepped old man Wisten, and nearly barreled into the wagon holding innkeeper Jollos and his celebratory cask of spring ale. A strong hand gripped him. He tried to wrench free but his pursuer hung on gamely. Hieronymus swung his arm around to knock the man loose but stumbled and felt himself falling. His assailant landed atop him heavily, driving the air from him.

For a moment he saw a ghostly site, not the man grappling him, but the village itself. The buildings appeared taller, more delicate in a shape, constructed of a black wood he didn't recognize, and carved with intricate designs that looped and swirled and intertwined into beautiful and strange rhythms. Just for a second, then it was gone, and his head beat like a club. It was too much. Hieronymus' panic drained away and anger took its place.

Why were they doing this?

All the frustration in his life stretched before him. His inability to travel the world to see exciting things, his parents understanding indifference, the constant headaches that leeched at his energy and drained his will, working on a fishing boat day after day, doomed to live in tiny village where nothing ever happened, his inability to express himself to Fulimera. And now this? Commanded to present himself by two men who scared him more than drowning. It was too much.

The grizzled stranger dragged him to his feet and growled menacingly, "Stop running boy."

Hieronymus screamed out his frustration and rage.

The man jerked back in surprise at Hieronymus' furious expression. The ale cask exploded with a booming noise. Golden ale sprayed everywhere and splintered remnants slammed into the man's head. With rolling glazed eyes, the man's grip slipped and fell away as he slid to the ground.

Hieronymus wiped foam from his face. His entire torso was soaked, and he shivered in the chilly dampness as ale dripped from his hair. Innkeeper Jollos stared in bewilderment at the splintered remains of his cask. People nearby sputtered and wrung the amber liquid from their clothes. The entire festival came to a lurching halt with expressions of surprise and confusion.

"Come on!" Kaevan jerked at Hieronymus' arm.

Hieronymus continued to stand, stunned at the sudden turn of events. His rage was gone, replaced by a sick feeling of shame at his lack of control. Dimly he was aware of the crowd's attitude shifting, from confusion to irritation that their celebration had been interrupted. His head started up and he saw Fulimera's shocked expression as she helped a soaked Ambri to her feet.

"Run!"

He stumbled after Kaevan. In four steps, they jumped some sitting benches and slipped past the dripping carving of Aellissea and her offerings, then disappeared into the shadows between Himmul's cobbler shop and the village meeting hall. Confused questions rose behind them but they paid no heed. Soon they were lost in the spindly maze of trees that bordered Braewickinn with only the sounds of their heavy breathing around them.

With the village far behind them and no pursuit in sight or sound they slowed, picking their way through the vegetation until they found a clearing nestled between two hillocks. There they collapsed and stared at each other in dull bewilderment.

"Well, everyone will remember this festival," said Kaevan.

Hieronymus smiled weakly at his friends attempt at cheering him up.

"And Jollos' keg, exploding like that." Kaevan smirked at the memory. "Bet he won't use that recipe again, way too strong." Then he grimaced. "Course, he might blame my Da for selling him a flawed cask."

Hieronymus nodded and said nothing. It was like a Skar Doorishmurk tale coming true, that cask exploding when it did. Because of that, he was free.

"Why did they want you?"

"How do I know?" Hieronymus snapped. He removed his shirt and hung it on a nearby brush to dry. The smell of ale was making him nauseous.

"Maybe you did something." Kaevan poked idly at his swollen lip.

Hieronymus shrugged. "You were there. They just came at me. What was I supposed to do?"

Kaevan nodded in agreement. "Evil looking bastards."

"How about you? That one hit you pretty hard."

"You know me, I always get back up."

"They weren't bothering anyone else. I wonder why?"

"We should see Thorath," said Kaevan.

Thorath was responsible for maintaining the peace in Braewickinn and the surrounding area. He once spent time as a caravan guard which was all the qualifications the village council needed to appoint him warden.

"Against those two? He wouldn't stand a chance."

Kaevan slumped, "True."

Hieronymus slipped his shirt back on. It was still damp and chilled now from the night air. Still, he felt better having it on again. "I'm going home."

Kaevan jumped up, "You can't!"

"Why not?"

"What if they're looking for you? Everyone knows who you are. The first place they'll look is your Da's house. Nope, you can't go back there. Not now."

Kaevan was right. His height made him too easy to track down. He needed another place to stay, but where?

"The boat then," Hieronymus asked.

"Nope, too obvious."

"I'll need to hide until they leave."

Kaevan grinned. "I know just the place."

"Where?"

"Follow me."

Kaevan led him on a roundabout route that eventually ended at the back of his father's crafting shop. It was where the two of them turned raw lumber into barrels, casks, and other containers used by the villagers. Hieronymus was a frequent visitor during the day but had never at night. The darkness gave everything a more sinister aura. The scent of cut timber, grated sawdust, cooling coal, charred wood, burnt iron and sweat hung in the air like a fog. Kaevan led him slowly through the shop, and then demonstrated he should climb a wooden ladder fastened to a rear wall.

Hieronymus clambered slowly upward and soon found himself in a small loft littered with crates and old tools. The roof was low and Hieronymus was forced to stoop low to avoid the beams crossing the ceiling. In one corner a heap of straw beckoned. He turned as Kaevan rose behind him with a pair of saddle blankets that he tossed at him.

"Da never uses it anymore so no one will think to look." Kaevan glanced around fondly. "Used to hide up here as a kid and imagine I was someplace else."

"You never told me."

Kaevan looked embarrassed. "It was my place, private."

Hieronymus nodded. "I understand."

"Just stay here, okay? I'll see what the mood is tomorrow and come get you once it's safe."

"Right."

"Night then." Kaevan disappeared down the ladder. Hieronymus watched his friend make his way unerringly across the crowded shop floor, peek carefully outside, then slip away.

Hieronymus sighed, the night had not turned out as expected. Instead of spending time with Fulimera, he was hiding in a loft from strangers who wanted him badly enough to cause a disturbance at the annual festival. He wondered if warder Thorath had faced up to them at all. Not the bravest of men was warden Thorath.

Hieronymus settled down, one blanket padding the loft floor, the other wrapped around him for warmth, the scent of horses soothing his tired emotions. His shirt was almost completely dry now and he relaxed into the warm scratchy blanket. As he drifted into sleep, he realized his headache was gone for the first time in days.

Hieronymus dreamed. He wasn't alone in the dark, there was a presence there, some being that he couldn't identify. It frightened him. A soft shuffle and it was standing behind him, close enough he imagined its breath tickling his neck hairs. He was too terrified to turn around, afraid of what might be lurking there, yet knew he must. He licked his parched lips, and spun. There was nothing there! He spun again, desperate for a glimmer, a confirmation that his fear was not of his imagination. A sudden weight smashed into him and he struggled to escape the woolly constriction of the horse blanket.

"Got'em," said a raspy voice.

Hieronymus' eyes popped open. No dream, this was real.

In the dim flickering light, he recognized the strangers from the village square. One had a gruesomely swollen and bruised face, the other mean-eyed and strong, both were now painfully holding his arms.

He struggled to tear himself free but they efficiently bound his hands together with leather wraps. Using callused hands and the threat of a sharp blade they forced him down the ladder. As soon as he was on the floor, the mean-eyed man kicked his feet away, leaving him prostrate and gasping with shock on the disturbed dust raised from the grimy floor.

How had they found him? How?

A slim silhouette approached from the doorway.

"There you are," said the woman in satisfaction.

She wasn't sullen anymore, now she looked like a cat eyeing trapped prey. A half-smile twisted her face. She was older than he had thought upon first seeing her. Shoulder length hair pulled back with silvery combs, matching the necklace hung from around her neck. She had a narrow chin and nose separated by thin lips, with dark eyes that studied him in annoyance. Her wide forehead was marked with a strange symbol, a circle with a slash angled through the right side. Hieronymus didn't recognize it.

"You've caused me a bit of trouble," she said. "And Reynald doesn't like you either." The swollen faced man glared down and spat next to Hieronymus' head in agreement. "Run again and I'll let him teach you a lesson. One you won't like at all."

"Who are you?"

"You can call me Lady Ilarhia. You've met Reynald, and over there is Derrend." She examined him closely and smirked without showing any teeth. "I find things. I'm very good at it and now I've found you."

Hieronymus worked some of the dryness from his mouth. "What do you want?"

The woman laughed quietly.

"Isn't that obvious? I want you."

"Me?"

"Actually, the Nimbus wants you. I'm simply the one good enough to find you." She looked at the younger man. "Derrend, get our mounts and another for him. Make sure you get the supplies. I want to be away from this stinking village well before dawn."

"Yes, Huntress." The mean-eyed man left. Reynald scowled down at Hieronymus, his face looking even more distorted and monstrous in the flickering torchlight.

Hieronymus had no idea what she was talking about. *Nimbus? Who or what was that?*

"You can't do this."

"I'm doing it. You're worth too much to ignore." She grinned wickedly. "They want you alive, and because of that I won't give you to Reynald."

He swallowed a lump in his throat and inwardly cowered.

"Where are we going?"

Lady Ilarhia straightened up, her bantering tone gone. "Gag him, we've getting out of here." Reynald cut a strip of Hieronymus' shirt and stuffed it into his mouth painfully. Another leather cord held it in place. Hieronymus stared wildly around seeking help. There was no one there.

She grabbed his chin with ringed fingers and glared at him from inches away. "Any more trouble and we'll set this pig sty of a village to flames. You understand?"

Hieronymus nodded slowly. The quiet venom in her voice had left no doubt in his mind that she would do it. He tried not to think of his mother or Fuli caught in the flames.

The soft clopping of hooves sounded outside.

"Let's go," the Huntress said.

The Lady Ilarhia strode away with a jaunty step. Reynald jerked Hieronymus to his feet and pushed him to follow. He stumbled along weakly, utterly confused and dispirited.

Derrend was outside astride one mount with three more trailing behind. One was a dun colored mare that looked suspiciously like the mayors favorite. All wore saddles and tack with large loosely wrapped bundles resting on their haunches. A glow of golden light rimmed the horizon as Aellissea would soon be rising to start a new day.

Hieronymus didn't get a chance to see anything more. Within minutes he was forced onto the mare, his hands bound to the saddle horn and another short rope passed beneath to bind his legs.

"Run boy, an see what happens," Reynald said as he checked Hieronymus' bonds.

The Lady Ilarhia and Reynald mounted and slowly walked their mounts to the edge of the village following Derrend. Once there they increased the pace until the dark strip of road underneath fairly flew by. He pulled fitfully at his bonds without success before slumping in defeat. Hieronymus bounced painfully in the saddle until exhaustion wore him down and he relaxed into the mare's swaying gait.

Aellissea was shining high in the sky before they slowed again. In the bright daylight Hieronymus realized he was in unfamiliar territory. The strangers had fled south out of Braewickinn and were now following a road Hieronymus had never trod before. All his other journeys had taken him north toward Brularn with his father. He knew Duer-lorn lay about a week away to the south but had never been there.

His captors continued riding and before long the events of last night, his lack of sleep, and the gentle swaying of his mount pulled Hieronymus into a restless doze.

Hieronymus awoke as they left the main road and angled into a copse of trees to their left. Once hidden within, his captors dismounted and spent some time stretching their legs, ignoring him completely. His whole body ached. He had never ridden for this long or this far and now his thighs and buttocks were stiff and chafed by the endeavor. In addition, he needed to piss terribly.

Finally, Derrend released the rope from around his legs and motioned him to get down. Hieronymus fell to the ground as his stiff legs refused to hold him up. New tingling aches poured through his body as the blood resumed its normal routes. He staggered up and weaved his way toward the closest tree and release. When he finished, he felt better. As he turned, Derrend struck him again.

Stunned Hieronymus gulped for air through his nose and gag as he lay, shook by the sudden violence.

Derrend loomed over him sneering. "That's for pissing in sight of a lady."

Reynald let out a laugh. The Lady Ilarhia ignored them all as she watched the horses nibble at the tall grass. If she had seen Hieronymus relieving himself she gave no indication.

"Get up."

Hieronymus struggled up and walked to where Reynald was building a small fire. Derrend pointed and Hieronymus sat, wary of further violence as the man roughly removed his gag.

The Lady Ilarhia approached. "How far?"

"Maybe a dozen miles, we made good time."

"Will they follow?"

Derrend shook his head. "The villagers? For him? Not likely, I grabbed the best horse there and set the rest free. Even if they decide to follow we've still got miles on them."

"You won't get away with this," said Hieronymus.

"It speaks," said Reynald.

"Of course we will," said the Huntress. She brushed a loose hair back from her face. "You're just a boy, not worth fighting for. Your family will be upset but what can they do? The rest are thankful we didn't take more and go back to their dreary lives. By next season they won't even remember you."

Hieronymus felt his stomach churn acidly. It wasn't true. His family cared, they would look for him, and his best friend Kaevan, he'd come after him too. Fulimera would miss him, wouldn't she? They did not know Braewickinners at all. They might not be the most prosperous village along the Opal coast but their determination and resilience to hardship was well known. His friends and family would come for him. He knew it.

"Eat," said Reynald. The bruised man passed him a biscuit and some strips of dried meat as well as a battered cup filled with hot *kaffe*. Hieronymus struggled to hold them without spilling or dropping anything. He realized he was starving. *How long since his last meal?* He couldn't remember.

The meat was dry, hard to chew, and so bland tasting there was no chance in figuring out what type of animal it had come from. The biscuit was like sun-dried mud and he nearly cracked a tooth on his first bite. The *kaffe* was hot, weak, and might have been made with dishwater for the dirty flavor it carried. Hieronymus ate it all ravenously.

By the time he finished, Reynald was kicking dirt over the fire erasing all evidence of its presence. Derrend collected the horses and rebound Hieronymus to his mount as the Lady Ilarhia sat looking back northward. Without a word, she turned and led them back to the road and headed south at a brisk pace. The rest of the day was spent alternating the horses between trotting and walking and putting as much distance between them and any pursuers as possible. When they stopped for the night Hieronymus was aching everywhere, his inner thighs afire and his mind restless with worry. He barely noticed that dinner was the same dried meat and biscuit meal before dropping into a dreamless sleep.

Derrend kicked him awake the next morning and after a brief breakfast, this time of boiled pottage, Hieronymus staggered to his mount without encouragement, suffered the indignity of being bound again and they were away.

More alert now Hieronymus watched his captors carefully. The three were obviously used to working together. Lady Ilarhia was definitely in command, as the two men obeyed her every instruction willingly if not with dispatch. Reynald the experienced campaigner seemed to be in charge of supplies and food preparation while Derrend took care of their mounts and guarded Hieronymus. Since grabbing him in the shop they had hardly spoken at all, each falling into routine so smoothly Hieronymus almost didn't notice it.

They walked the horses today as if confident of no pursuit, crossing a series of low hills alternating between tall grasslands and the occasional hedges and woods that covered the area. Once Hieronymus saw smoke from what could have been a distant farmstead but it quickly passed out of sight behind the tall branches of another wood. As the miles passed, Hieronymus couldn't take the silence anymore.

Hesitantly he asked, "Where are you taking me?"

"Duer-lorn for now," said Lady Ilarhia.

Hieronymus resisted his sudden excitement. A city! After years of dreaming he would finally get to see one. Being forced there against his will had not been part of those dreams. "Is it bigger than Brularn?"

She rolled her eyes. "Much."

"Why are you doing this? To me, I mean. What have I done to you? Why me?"

The Lady Ilarhia laughed as a ringed finger slid a stray hair back into place. "Its what we do, find people like you and turn them over to Nimbus."

"Like me?" Hieronymus frowned in confusion. "What about me?"

She shook her head in amusement.

"He don't know," said Reynald. The swelling on his face had receded but the bruising was an angry mottle of yellows, greens, and blues.

"Oh, he's a rare one all right. It should have taken him years ago. How old are you boy?"

Something should have taken him? What were they talking about?

Hieronymus said. "Fifteen winters." He wished he could rub his forehead as he felt another headache coming on, but his bound hands prevented it. "What should have taken me?"

"Maybe we made a mistake," said Derrend.

"No, it's him," said the Lady Ilarhia. "I can feel him now, right here." She pointed to her own forehead and peered at Hieronymus. "You feel it too."

Hieronymus blinked in surprise. *She could feel his headache? Was that what she was talking about? His headaches!*

"My head throbs sometimes, so what? Everyone gets headaches now and then."

"Oh it throbs all right, just before it drills into your mind like lances at the charge, until agony is all you know and all you can do is scream it away." Her eyes bored into Hieronymus daring him to deny her descriptions of his episodic and painful experiences. With a shock, he realized he couldn't.

"What is it?" He whispered.

"That's why Nimbus wants you," said Lad Ilarhia. "I'll let them explain it once they've paid our finders fee." He heard Reynald and Derrend chuckle at the prospect.

Hieronymus worried at the Huntress' revelation like a starving dog over a meaty bone. They wanted him for his headaches? It made no sense

His headaches had started a couple of years previously, at first just a dull ache that ebbed and flowed, sometimes almost gone, more often just annoying and continuous. His mother had taken him to the local herb woman who gave him some crushed medicine that if steeped in tea was supposed to make them go away. It had worked for a time but they always came back. Most days his headaches were just there, a dull throbbing in the back of head like the pounding surf. Sometimes, like at the festival they had been distracting and painful. Seldom were the pain and blood pulsing gone.

However, his headache had gone and not an herb in sight. It had left him as he had grappled with Reynald in the square. No, that wasn't true, not while they were fighting. It disappeared as he screamed out his frustrations at his dreary life.

The Lady Ilarhia could somehow sense his headaches. Hieronymus had never heard of such a thing. *Had she guessed?* Not likely. His head had been throbbing when she had pointed at him in Braewickinn and again when it was barely noticeable to himself. She hadn't guessed, she knew. But how? Did it have something to do with that mark?

His headaches were important to someone, otherwise why kidnap him. But what did they mean?

"How many others have you captured for Nimbus?"

Lady Ilarhia shrugged. "A few," she said. "Not many really. The failures quite outweigh the successes. But you, you are a success. The Nimbus will be happy to get you."

"But, what have I got?"

She sniffed, smiled at some private thought and moved her horse away.

"What have I got?" Hieronymus looked at Reynald and Derrend in desperation. "What am I?" Both ignored him.

That night Reynald managed to snare a rabbit and all of them ate something other than pottage, travel biscuits and meat.

Hieronymus sat staring at the random sparks that shot into the night sky from the snapping fire, his thoughts as fleeting as they were. His headache was back, a quiet presence lurking just below his awareness.

It had to be a mistake. Why would anyone care whether his head hurt or not? It made no sense and the more he tried to find an answer the more it slipped away like an eel. Did Ilarhia experience the same pains? Was that how she knew of his?

It was so frustrating, this not knowing. He could feel his heart beating harder and the veins in his head pulsing as he clenched his jaw to avoid crying out. If only he dared to howl. Then maybe the pain would go away again like it did when the cask exploded.

Hieronymus froze.

Right after the cask exploded!

Hieronymus rocked gently back and forth, as he strove to remember the exact order of events. Reynald jerking him upward, the fear he felt being manhandled like a child, the sense of danger unlike any he had ever known. His thoughts on all the disappointing events and wearying circumstances and dashed expectations he had experienced. He remembered the sudden rage that overwhelmed him and his full-bodied scream at the futility of his life and the cask bursting like a melon with the sound like a crack of lightning striking a nearby tree.

The cask had not exploded after he screamed; it had exploded as he screamed.

Was that it? Had he been the one to burst it open?

If he were the one that caused the cask to burst, it would explain why Lady Ilarhia and Nimbus wanted him so badly. He stopped rocking.

The thought shriveled him to his soul. If he had burst the cask, then he was in more danger than he had ever imagined.

He was a magic user!

He knew the legends; he learned them from his mother as she taught him to read using the few ancient well cared for books and rolled parchments that Braewickinn owned. Magic disappeared from Bulinnärm thousands of years before when *Illishimeer*, the enchanted *alfr* city was destroyed. For centuries thereafter, magic users had been hunted to extinction by the fearful remnants of civilizations that survived *Illishimeer's* fall.

The frightening tales of their destruction had often kept the child Hieronymus up late into the night. There was Mad Elcutt, famous for collecting the tongues of magic users and carrying them around his neck as a necklace; the Blackstahl Knight who's mighty hammer once killed four of them before they could cast a single spell; the flaming screaming pyres as frightened kingdoms exterminated them all in a frenzy of fear. Hieronymus shivered at the gruesome fates magic users had suffered. Now Bulinnärm was free of their powers and few wished for their return.

Lady Ilarhia was a hunter, but why would she be looking for him? How would they even know?

There was only one answer: she could sense the power inside him, that's what she did. That's how she knew. While he thought his headaches were normal he now knew they were portended extreme danger for him. Something, that if true, would make him a pariah throughout the empires and kingdoms and lands of the Three Realms.

Someone whom everybody would want to kill.

A hand covered his mouth. Hieronymus jerked awake ready to fight but then saw who it was. *Kaevan*, he mouthed beneath the hand. His friend nodded slowly and then removed his hand.

Hieronymus looked around. Reynald snored nearby; his feet close to the remnants of fire. Beyond him, Hieronymus could see the rounded hip of Lady Ilarhia as she lay under a silken blanket. A restless horse snorted nearby. Where was Derrend?

Kaevan was urging him up. Hieronymus extended his arms to show his bindings. With a grimace, Kaevan drew his blade and sawed through the leather bonds. Carefully Hieronymus exposed his feet and pointed at the bonds around his ankles. Kaevan looked exasperated but cut them as well.

As silently as he could Hieronymus rose and followed Kaevan. His legs felt weak from riding and his head swiveled endlessly seeking the missing Derrend. He followed his friend away from the camp for several hundred steps until they came upon a pair of waiting horses. For the first time in days, Hieronymus felt a sense of relief. His friend had come for him.

A wide smile flashed on Kaevan's face in the scattered moonslight of mighty *Lindruuth* as he chased the goddess *Lystennielle* across the night sky.

Hieronymus embraced his friend in gratitude, overcome with emotion. He relented when Kaevan began beating on his back for air.

"Kaevan, how?"

"Easy, Starling leaves a pretty good trail."

Starling! The mayors mare was named Starling.

"Where's everyone else?"

"They think you ran away. Figured you return once with your tail twixt your legs once you got hungry. They wouldn't listen to me. So I followed you."

"I didn't know you could track."

"Learned it searching for trees to cut into barrels." Kaevan turned to untie a set of reins. "Let's go, before they know your gone."

"But I already know," said a voice from the darkness.

Hieronymus and Kaevan froze. He knew that voice.

Derrend stepped into the clearing his sword point held threateningly low. "You should have stayed home kid. Might have lived a long life there."

Kaevan shoved Hieronymus towards a horse. "Ride!"

The next moments were a jumble of fear-induced activity as Hieronymus fought to scramble atop a horse. Astride he turned to see Kaevan circling away from the armed man with one arm hanging loosely at his side and Derrend closing in with upraised sword. Hieronymus kicked and his mount jumped forward. Before the villain could avoid it, the huge barrel chest knocked him sprawling. Frantically Hieronymus pulled the horse's head around to keep the fallen man in sight. Kaevan appeared next to him astride the other mount and urged in a hoarse voice. "Go!"

Together the two raced into the night and away from the cursing Derrend.

Hieronymus did not know how long they rode wildly. With every mile, he felt the fear loosening inside. He was free. He could not remember feeling anything like this before, the exaltation, the sense of relief and joy in having escaped his watchdogs and Lady Ilarhia.

He grinned broadly as he thought of her reaction as Derrend reported his escape. He was about to share it when Kaevan fell from his mount.

"Kaevan?"

Hieronymus reined his mount to a stop and threw himself down. He ignored his weak legs and scrambled over to his friends jumbled form. He rolled Kaevan over to see a gaping wound and nearly severed arm. He blanched at the sight.

"No, no, no." He did not recognize his own voice in his sudden panic. He had to think what to do, and he did. He had to stop the bleeding. He wrenched his shirt off and began tearing strips of cloth from it. He could feel tears forming as he wrapped the ghastly wound.

Kaevan moaned and one hand flayed in the air for support. Hieronymus gripped it firmly and saw his friends gaze lock on his.

"Messed that up," Kaevan whispered.

"No, no, you did great," Hieronymus said.

Kaevan coughed weakly, then grinned a macabre smile. "At least we're away from Braewickinn."

Hieronymus chuckled despite himself. "Yeah, we are."

Kaevan blinked slowly. With a serious expression he said, "You can't return, first place they'll look."

Hieronymus nodded. "I know."

His friend's head lolled back, and then he drew on some inner strength and glared at Hieronymus. "Journey," he said. A thin strand of blood leaked from his mouth and trailed across his chin and neck. "See it all, okay?"

"I will," Hieronymus whispered. Tears rolled down his cheeks endlessly. "I'll visit Choy, Worldheart, from Kist to mighty Alexiandrölarn itself. All those places we dreamt of visiting, I'll see the all."

"Do it, for both of us," Kaevan whispered, and then he was gone.

He buried Kaevan on a small hillock near a large oak tree. He was sure his boyhood friend would appreciate the view.

He looked north toward Braewickinn. He dare not go back. His mother would never know what happened to him, his father toiling away at sea alone, and of course, Fulimera's enchanting smile. It would be too dangerous to return now. Someday, maybe he would, but not this day.

Hieronymus had found his dream and Kaevan had died making it possible. He needed to wander the world now, making his own way while avoiding other hunters from Nimbus. He needed to learn more about his power and how to control it. Once he did, he would seek out Nimbus, and he would get his answers.

Duer-lorn is that way, he thought, *Beyond that was the entire world.*

He went searching for his wandering horse.

A Lesson in Power

Foreword

Almost immediately after finishing The Huntress I decided to continue the story of young Hieronymus and began work on its follow-up, A Lesson in Power. I wanted to explore Hieronymus' life as he grew into his power, and do it using a series of short stories that comprised a small part of a larger tale. So far it seems to be working. I'm learning at the same pace Hieronymus is, which makes it both exciting and nerve racking. As the author I recognize it all has to make sense but I'm writing the individual episodes as a pantser, i.e., someone who makes it up as they write. I know the goal, but how I get there is totally up to chance at this point. What fun!

Cold drops of rain wormed their way past the tightly drawn collar, chilling him to the bone. Hieronymus hunched his shoulders and shivered. He shook wet dangling strands of hair out of his face and peered through the driving rain for any sign of shelter. He was alone, cold, hungry, hunted.

Moreover, lost as well.

His cloak was not designed for hard travel, doing little to protect him from the wind and rain. A better cloak was the farthest thing from his mind in the middle of an escape attempt. He flinched at the memory. Kaevan guiding him away from Lady Ilarhia control after days of captivity, the frenzied race to freedom, and the bitter taste of that victory, Kaevan's death.

He shook his head again; unsure if it were rain or tears he flung away. He used a wet sleeve to wipe his nose and patted his mount in reassurance.

"There's shelter here somewhere," he said. He urged his mount to a walk. "Let's find it."

He was following a faint trail he hoped would lead where he wanted to go, the city of Duer-lorn. He knew it lay somewhere to the southeast and several riding days away but after hours in the pouring rain, he was no longer sure which direction his plodding mount walked. The heavy canopy overhead prevented him from seeing the sun, just as it had hidden the coming deluge.

Another shiver shook his gaunt frame, his thin garments soaked through completely. The water had even dripped into his boots as he squeezed water from between chilled toes.

He remembered his father teaching him numerous means of identifying their course while at sea. By sun and stars, by currents and wind, but on land, he felt lost. The brightness of *Aellissea* as she passed overhead helped, but he trusted the stars. With no one to ask in these bleak drizzly woods, he was relying on trader and merchant stories as his guide.

Hieronymus rode awkwardly, long legs dangling, hunched over and clutching the pommel in large knuckled hands to conserve body heat. He needed shelter, or a fire, or both. But he no idea how to find one or make the other. His teeth chattered in distress.

In all the tales he remembered, none mentioned hardships like this. Sure, there were dangerous storms, and savage beasts, and evil enemies to overcome, but heroes were seldom deterred from their goals. The mighty King Skar Doorishmurk never suffered from cold driving rain, nor had the heat sucked from his body by gusting winds like legendary vampires. True heroes did not suffer like this, did they?

Hieronymus sneezed, and then wiped away the rain dripping down his nose. He was no hero, not at all. He was just another lost traveller, battered by storm and in dire need of help.

Since escaping the Huntress, he preferred the loneliness of winding trails through the woods to exposing himself on the trade road. He may be a villager far from familiar territory, but not a fool. He knew she would seek him there first.

Besides, he knew generally where Duer-lorn was located and was confident he could make it there when first he escaped. In the current downpour, he was no longer sure. In addition, Duer-lorn would be the last place Lady Ilarhia would look for him. While the Huntress searched elsewhere, he hoped it would give him time to learn more about his power and the nature of Nimbus.

That is, unless Nimbus found and killed him first.

Hieronymus shivered at the thought. Only days before he was cursing his boring life as a fisher. Now, he was on the run, unable to return home, hunted for possessing a power he neither understood nor controlled, and one which brought the possessor a death sentence.

And claimed the life of his best friend Kaevan.

His mount stepped into a fierce wind from the safety of the trees. It tore at his garments and the creaking branches overhead. A shallow valley with wind ruffled grasses stretched before him, ending at the base of an ancient stone keep that had seen better centuries. Neatly tilled gardens lay before it, a narrow winding track pointing at a stout gate entrance. He squinted but could see no pennants, nor movement on the wall or smoke drifting from a lone chimney.

Hieronymus sneezed again. It did not look welcoming, but it might be dry.

He kneed his mount forward and crossed the glistening wet clearing. The rain bore down on him in torrents, creating a multitude of watery streams flowing across the uneven ground. The wind tore at his thin cloak with demonic determination as if angered at his attempt to seek shelter.

The keep looked even worse as he got closer. Vines grew up the lichen covered wall spreading upward almost to the peak. The stones themselves were pocked and ancient looking, darkened by the rain, yet still solid and unyielding. The gate was bleached gray from weathering, thick and imposing, with iron straps pitted with age.

Evidence of occupation became more obvious as he approached, the tilled gardens showing signs of recent hoeing and cutting. Even so, no hail greeted his approach.

Stiff with cold, Hieronymus slipped to the mud before the gate and pounded on the wooden beams. His fist made dull thumping noises barely audible over the downpour. Rain stung his cheeks as he stood and waited. When no one replied he pushed against the gate, the vague hope of it being unlatched quickly dashed.

"Hello!" He squinted upward against the rain. He drew a knife and used it to knock again. The sounds were much louder. "Is anyone there?"

He sneezed again. He had to find shelter, and soon. Maybe there was a shed or lean-to nearby he could use. He turned to leave when there was a shriek of metal against metal, then half of the gate swung back. The darkness inside beckoned.

Relieved he had been heard, Hieronymus murmured a short prayer of thanks to *Aellissea* before leading his mount inside.

Three shadowy figures stood watching him intently in the tiny yard. The courtyard did not protect against the rain but the rapacious wind could still be heard wailing overhead. Hieronymus stood and waited, examining them in turn.

The closest was an elderly man; thin as a rail, wearing a thick woolen robe, a plain rope around his waist, and open sandals that squelched in the mud. He was nearly bald, with a high forehead and wiry hair encircling his head like a gray briar patch. He kept his distance from Hieronymus, waiting until he was well inside before hurriedly closing and barring the gate.

The others were dressed in a similar manner.

A younger version of the gate opener stood nearby. He had the same high forehead but a full head of hair, plastered close to his skull by the rain. Unlike the elder, he was pointing the tines of a pitchfork toward Hieronymus in a threatening manner. His eyes blinked rapidly in the rain as he watched Hieronymus, a serious expression on his face, while shuffling nervously side to side.

Hieronymus sneezed and the young man jumped.

"Settle Kuulman," said the third man.

The third man held a cudgel and ignored the rain dripping from his frizzled curled hair. His was a strong bony face with sad expressive eyes, and a wide mouth with lips which moved constantly in and out as he took in Hieronymus' drenched and shabby appearance. He stood at medium height and had a stocky build covered in a plain robe and sandals with an easy attitude Hieronymus recognized as someone of authority. Finally, he seemed to reach a decision and spoke.

"You look like shit, boy. Are you lost?"

Hieronymus opened his mouth but a shiver racked his tall frame and all he could manage was to shake his head.

"You don't look dangerous, more like a drowned raccoon, not that I've ever seen one so big. Let's get you inside before you fall down." He gestured at Hieronymus' mount. "Kuulman, tend to the lad's horse. Guri, gather some dry clothes."

He turned and marched away. "Come on boy, inside."

Hieronymus followed him gratefully. Inside he found a short stone hallway with several arched openings along the walls and a pair of lamps glowing brightly. He left a dripping trail as the man gestured him into a narrow room decorated with paintings, well-carved female statuettes, and old but well maintained wood furniture. A fire blazed merrily away in the large fireplace at the end of the room. Hieronymus could feel its warmth from across the room.

He quickly doffed his dripping cloak and at a gesture from the man dropped it to the stone floor in a sodden heap. Gratefully he spread his hands and basked in the heat emanating from the fire. He heard the rain beating faintly on the roof, distant and almost forgotten as he willed the chills from his body. Wisps of steam soon forced him to back away as the man Guri returned and handed him a rough towel and some dry clothes.

"I'll be right back," said the stocky man.

Without a word, Hieronymus stripped off his wet garments, rubbed himself dry and hurriedly donned the offered clothes. They were short in the arms and legs but fit well around his shoulders and waist. Hieronymus did not care. They were dry and a welcome change. Guri hung his wet garments from a hastily strung line before the fireplace.

Warmed and with his nose no longer dripping, Hieronymus had to admit he felt better. Soon, the stocky man returned with a tray of crusty bread and a bowl filled with hot vegetable broth. Hieronymus accepted it gratefully, sat, and soon his insides felt as warm as his exterior. The man watched him eat closely without saying a word.

"Thank you," said Hieronymus.

"You're welcome," said the man. "*Mrynlinn* states that 'one should strive to make new friends every day, else find themselves friendless when in need.'"

"I like that," said Hieronymus. "Who's *Mrynlinn*?"

"She is the sister of *He Who Seeks to Know*."

Hieronymus looked around the room. All of the painting held the same woman, one with an oval face, soft and expressive eyes, full lips, black hair, and surrounded by a halo of golden-green light. Her eyes hinted at hidden knowledge, her form swathed in translucent robes of teal and silver which both obscured and revealed the womanly form underneath. The statuettes also showed her standing in poses reminding Hieronymus of speakers and leaders.

His mother had drilled the major gods and goddesses into her children as was proper. He knew of *Aellissea, Lindruuth, Lystennielle, Kara, Shonsolu, Issyr*, and others, but never *Mrynlinn*.

"You worship her then?"

"Oh no, no one worships *Mrynlinn*, she hated that. We simply follow her teachings." The man smiled, his teeth were even. "My name is Merzeicsi. I'm Monszer of *Her* little sanctuary. We call it Duerlwood Priory. And you are?"

"Hieronymus, from Braewickinn village."

"The fishing village to the North? I've heard of it. What brings you to our little retreat?"

Hieronymus paused. He could not tell Monszer the real reason. That he was running from people who sought to kill him. The Monszer looked and acted like someone he could trust, but caution urged him to keep the knowledge to himself. He sputtered out the first thing that popped into his head.

"I have an uncle in Duer-lorn. I'm supposed to become his apprentice, but I got lost in the storm." He shrugged.

"All alone?" The Monszer tilted his head in puzzlement. "That's a long way for someone your age, wouldn't you agree Guri?"

The older man nodded solemnly. "A merchant run would have been much safer."

"Agreed, agreed."

Hieronymus leaned back in his chair, lids heavy. The room's warmth, the filling food, and the first friendly talk in days were making him sleepy. He yawned and heard his jaw crack in protest.

"I'm sorry," he mumbled.

From far away he heard Monszer's voice. "Don't worry, *Mrynlinn* will comfort you."

Hieronymus settled into the chair and began snoring softly.

Hieronymus startled awake. He was alone in the room, the once blazing fire now reduced to a cheerful bed of coals. The patter of rain no longer beat on the roof and Hieronymus was surprised how much better he felt. He must have slept for quite awhile.

"Hello?"

When no one answered, Hieronymus rose and found his formerly wet clothes washed and neatly folded on a nearby stool. Another tray of thick crusty bread, velvety slabs of cheese, and some sliced sausage waited next to them. His stomach growled at the sight and without thinking he started in on the tasty repast. A pitcher of water completed the meal.

Hieronymus wiped away the last crumbs. "Hello? Is anyone here?"

He walked into the hallway, now lit by sunlight trailing through the open door. The shadowy hall Hieronymus from yesterday now shone with the warm tones of polished woodwork, still old and worn, but well maintained. Tapestries hung between the doors, faded now, but showing signs of their former color and greatness.

Hieronymus slowly walked down the hall examining each tapestry in silence. His mother would have been impressed with the workmanship and attention to detail. He glanced into each archway as he passed. To his left was another great room, with long tables and stools capable of seating dozens, and a raised platform at the end draped with colorful hangings of teal and silver trim. The last archway revealed a stone stairwell leading to the upper floors.

However, the final archway drew Hieronymus' attention. Inside were more books than he thought existed in the world? Hundreds of volumes stood in shelves along each wall, while others rested atop wide tables, or stacked in piles within reach of comfortable looking reading chairs. Amazed at the treasure trove of knowledge in front of him, Hieronymus wandered inside and let his eyes stray over the titles.

There was a leather bound volume called *Secrets of the Alfr*, and on another table a *History of the Three Realms; From the Fall of Illishimeer to the Rise of Alexiandrölarn* inside a lacquered cover of white wood. Near it rested *Tribes of the Owixi* with a cover made of tree bark. A tiny blue bound book called *Fables of the True Gods and* a giant tome declared itself *The Complete Collected Tales of King Skar Doorishmurk*, as told by Master Bard Aluju. Hieronymus carefully ran a finger up and down the soft leather binding. He thought he knew many of Skar's stories, but here was a book claiming to hold them all.

All around him waited books of history, anthologies of stories, biographies, treatises, tomes, scrolls, and parchments covering more subjects than Hieronymus ever imagined. He wandered the room in awe, every title and author he found more amazing than the previous.

"Do you read?"

Hieronymus jumped. Monszer Merzeicsi stood in the doorway wearing a wide hat, carrying a garden hoe, and a smile on his face.

Hieronymus nodded, afraid to speak and break the sense of wonderment he felt. He stroked a finger across one embossed cover. "How?"

"*Mrynlinn's* will," said Merzeicsi. "*She* values information and books to spread knowledge. As her disciples, we devote our life to doing so."

"I never imagined," said Hieronymus. "You have so many."

Merzeicsi laughed and lazily swept a hand around. "This? This is nothing. A humble collection of *Her* will. The library of Alexiandrölarn, now there is a collection."

Hieronymus tried to imagine so much knowledge in one place and failed. His village contained only a handful of books and those always under the constant care of adults. His mother taught him to read from one. He had taken to it like a fish to water, devouring every written word in the village until he could repeat them verbatim. A good part of his desire to explore the world was his desire to find and read more books. To find so much new knowledge in one place was a dream come true.

He hesitated, his finger lingering on a compendium of plants and animals of the realms. He licked his lips. "May I…"

"Read them? Of course, it's *Mrynlinn's* desire. Feel free to do so later. Right now, *Aellissea* shines, the day is gloriously clear, and weeds need pulling. Come."

Hieronymus let himself be led out of the fabulous room, thrilled at the opportunity to explore it.

Hieronymus followed Monszer outside where the others cleared weeds away from the tiny shoots poking their way through the finely broken soil.

"Here," said Kuulman. The young monk handed Hieronymus a hoe and pointed at the row next to him. Guri continued working as Monszer joined him.

"Thanks." Hieronymus joined in and the four worked quietly.

"King Holmgerjen," said Monszer.

"Young King Holmgerjen," said Kuulman, "was the first to unite his warring dukes with a common goal. The dukes Skor and Arnhandlar were constantly encroaching on the lands of their fellow dukes, Kaarspel, Laderskon and Barafisk. They allied with some dukes from other kingdoms using promises of land and wealth, but were constantly stymied by the weak support. It was during that time…"

Guri noticed Hieronymus' puzzled expression. "Have you heard of King Holmgerjen?"

Hieronymus shook his head.

"Sorry," said Kuulman, and looked chagrined. "King Holmgerjen ruled as a king over the largest number of dukedoms in northern Alexiandrömor prior to the emperors rise four centuries ago. Actually, his uniting of those dukedoms into kingdoms led to the creation of the Thousand Kingdoms and eventually the empire we know today."

"Kuulman is always a bit long-winded when it comes to history," said Monszer.

"But it's fascinating," said Kuulman.

"Yes, it is," said Monszer, "and you tell it well." He returned to weed pulling but continued speaking. "*Mrynlinn* wants knowledge to spread, so we do, even as we work. It helps time to pass and spreads our individual interests and knowledge to others, as we learn more about this world we walk." He laughed. "Its better than talking crops all the time, although we do that too."

Monszer, Guri, and Kuulman were the only occupants of Duerlwood Priory. They were disciples of the Order of *Mrynlinn*; a lesser goddess of knowledge esteemed across the Three Realms by bards, storytellers, librarians, scholars, philosophers and learned sages. They spent their lives collecting knowledge, recording it for others, and passing it on to everyone.

After toiling in the gardens, they ate a brief lunch before going indoors to a well lit room with scribing tables, parchment, and stacks of quills ready for use. There they spent the afternoon creating new copies of old manuscripts. As dusk arrived they enjoyed another meal and then everyone filed into the library and settled down for reading. Kuulman grabbed a thick tome and huddled in a pillowed alcove directly under a lamp and began reading. Guri sat in one of the reading chairs reading a miniscule volume bearing a title in a flowing embossed script incomprehensible to Hieronymus.

Hieronymus stood and stared. *Where to start?*

"Try this one," said Monszer. He handed Hieronymus a plain tome, tan in color, and titled *The Geography of Alexiandrömor*.

Hieronymus accepted the book gingerly, afraid of damaging it. He found a place to sit and tenderly opened it and began to read. It was not until Guri touched his shoulder did he notice how much time had passed. He closed the book and set it down, his head filled with the names of rivers, lakes, mountains, and other prominent geographical features. He had not imagined the world could be so large. Guri led him upstairs and waved him into a room where Kuulman already slept. A second bed awaited his tired body.

Hieronymus settled into the rhythm of life at the priory.

During the morning there were chores to do and everyone, including the Monszer, helped to gather firewood, weed and till the vegetable gardens, feed and water the few pigs, chickens, and turkeys kept by the retreat. In the afternoon, when the heat drove them indoors they sometimes worked on mending clothes, polishing and cleaning the keep, but mainly at translating older tomes into more common languages, something Hieronymus never heard of before, having only ever heard his native tongue.

"Oh no," laughed Monszer. "There are hundreds of tongues spoken across the Three Realms. The *dwarvulk* have one, the *alfr* another, the mountain clans of Worldheart have several, the tribes of Owixi hundreds more. One you reach Duer-lorn you'll hear them."

Everyone took turns making the meals. Hieronymus learned the rudiments of making bread from Guri and the best herbs and seasoning for creating tasty stews and soups from Kuulman. The Monszer tended to spice up his meals while Guri stuck to the basics.

Every night the four would gather in the library room and read until night was well upon them. The next day everyone took their turn at telling what they had learned the night before. Kuulman tended to read histories and could go on for hours on the lineages of various kingdoms and dynasties whether human, *Dwarvulk*, or *Alfr*. Guri loved ancient poets and philosophers and amazed Hieronymus by often reciting his favorites in their native tongue as well as arguing both sides of a philosophical position. The Monszer loved history as much as Kuulman but concentrated on the goods produced and traded between the kingdoms, the wars over precious resources, and the men and policies leading to the conflicts.

At first Hieronymus was reticent to join in their discussions, fearing his lack of knowledge made him look foolish. However, the Monszer would not allow it, insisting Hieronymus share something every day. Reluctant at first it soon dawned on him the retelling was aiding him in remembering the details of what he had learned. It also forced him to organize his thoughts better in order to relay them to others. Soon he was eager to share his new found information as they worked the gardens.

It was another sunny morning in the fields, among the growing vegetables and aromatic herbs when Hieronymus realized he was happy.

He still missed his family, and the pain of losing Kaevan was fading. But the simple chores, access to hundreds of books, and the vibrant conversations among like-minded people merged together and brought comfort to his troubled spirit. He would never forget his previous life but somehow sensed his path led elsewhere. He could not imagine where it would lead but he knew he could no longer join his father as a fisher.

He shifted to the next row and continued pulling weeds, a new lightness in his heart.

Did he have a chance?

For the last few weeks he had been free of headaches, the longest period he could remember. Since they had started most days the ache was a constant irritant, like a grumbling stomach, distracting but easy to ignore. Other times it throbbed for attention like a crying baby, unforgiving and remorseless. However, to have no pain at all was new, and he was not sure how to feel about it.

Was the power gone?

If he no longer had the power, would Lady Ilarhia still hunt for him? Would Nimbus still pay her to deliver him? If he were not a sorcerer, they would have no reason to kill him. It was all confusing, and without his friend Kaevan he had no one to share his thoughts or fears with.

Should he ask Monszer? The man in question was taking a short break, thirstily sipping water from a ladle. *Dare he?*

Hieronymus shook himself. *No, he could not.*

Many generations ago, ever since the Great Burning, sorcerers of all races and types were hunted down and destroyed. They were extinct, except in legend and fearsome tales told to frighten children into obedience, as his own mother once had. He knew he was not a sorcerer. How could he be? His family's roots were sunk deep into the rocky shore of Braewickinn. Everyone knew sorcerers were either *Alfr* or from royal family lines, not hardscrabble coastal fishermen.

However, convincing others seemed impossible. They would believe what they wanted.

He dug furiously at a deeply rooted clump of weeds.

If Monszer knew, what would he do?

Hieronymus did not know, nor did he wish to find out.

So far, the Monszer had not asked about his apprenticeship with his uncle, seemingly content to let Hieronymus speak first. He stopped weeding, suddenly regretting the earlier lies. Why should he believe Hieronymus now?

Had Lady Ilarhia given up her search? Was she still out there, looking for him? Maybe she was seeking other prey? Hieronymus could not guess. With the power gone, could she even find him?

Guri gave a whistle and automatically Hieronymus grabbed his weed filled basket and followed the others to the dumpsite. Gardening chores were over, time to move onto the scripting room after a brief repast.

Three days later, he awoke feeling uncomfortable. The swollen, continuous pounding of blood pulsing through his temples was back. Somehow, he made it through the morning chores, speaking little as Guri recounted tales of the *Dwarvulk* wars against the *Alfr*. Gardening completed they moved inside where Hieronymus barely nibbled his share of food.

"Riders!"

Kuulman's shout stopped them from entering the script room. He stood in the doorway and pointed outside. The Monszer strode past him into the courtyard. Hieronymus sidled up to the door and peeked out the narrow sliver between the door and its frame. Lady Ilarhia, Reynald and Derrend sat on their mounts in the tiny courtyard. All of them looked tired, travel stained, and irritated.

"Welcome to Duerlwood Priory," said Monszer. "Take a moment to relax and water your horses."

Lady Ilarhia nodded once, and then intoned, "Monszer, I thank you for the offer, but we're in a hurry. I'm seeking a tall youth. A dangerous runaway that's also a murderer. Have you seen him?"

Hieronymus swayed slightly and stopped breathing. The rays of light entering the keep was suddenly too bright, the gasp of Kuulman too loud as he glanced his way. After all this time, she was here, and still hunting.

"A murderer? That is terrible news."

"We've been charged with bringing him back for trial. Have you seen him?"

"No, no, we haven't," said Monszer. "We seldom get visitors here, or see strangers. Are you sure you won't take refreshment?"

Let them go! Hieronymus shouted silently inside his aching head. *Why was he talking to her?*

"I thank you for your offer, but I must refuse." The Lady Ilarhia signaled and all three turned their mounts and departed. Derrend cast a final look back before they exited the gate. The Monszer watched for a moment, then turned and strode purposely into the keep.

Kuulman backed away, eyes wide as he stared at Hieronymus.

"Come," said Monszer. "They're looking for *you*."

Hieronymus breathed deeply and silently followed.

Monszer stood near the banked fireplace, showing his back to Hieronymus with hands clasp together. The painted and carved images of *Mrynlinn* wore shaded expressions of disappointment as they gazed at him sightlessly. The Monszer rocked on his heels slightly as if fighting a strong breeze.

"I'm sorry…"

Monszer turned, a hand raised. "No, I'm sorry." He settled into a chair with a sigh and waited for Hieronymus to sit. "I had hopes. You obviously have the mind, untrained as it is now, to join us, or go even farther. Now I am not so sure. Is it true? Are you a runaway?"

"Only from her," said Hieronymus.

"Did you murder someone?"

Hieronymus was standing. "No, she's lying."

"Sit, sit, and tell me."

Hieronymus stumbled through the story as best he could. The arrival of the Lady Ilarhia and his kidnapping, his days of captivity, and then Kaevan's sudden appearance, rescue, and death. Tears flowed freely as he told of his final promise, and then the days of wandering until finding the priory.

The Monszer listened without interruption until the very end. He swept a hand through curly hair before asking, "Do you know why she hunts you?"

He swallowed as fear gripped him again. Could he tell Monszer of his suspicions? That he could be a sorcerer? Would Monszer believe him? If he did, what would he do? For centuries, the answer always meant death. No, as much as he trusted the Monszer, he could not answer that question.

"I don't know. She wouldn't tell me." Hieronymus dropped his eyes, his cheeks burning. He was ashamed of lying to someone who had sheltered him. "She wanted to deliver me to someone called Nimbus."

The Monszer's expression froze. "Nimbus?"

"You know of him?"

"It's not him, it's something more." He sat back and studied Hieronymus intently. His pondering interrupted by Kuulman's frantic arrival.

"Monszer, they're back."

The Monszer stiffened. The Monszer's gaze dart left and right as he furiously considered alternatives. He reached a decision, stood. "Stay here." He strode from the room shouting, "Guri!"

The throbbing in his head resumed, more insistent than before.

Could he still escape? The front gate was the only way out. To go into the courtyard would reveal he was here. *Could he hide?* No, they would take the priory apart looking for him. She would use her ability to find him.

Wait! She had not detected him before; maybe her abilities were not as strong or reliable as she had led him to believe. Maybe he could escape. He was suddenly standing in the hall again, with no memory of walking, listening to the confrontation outside.

"You will turn Hieronymus over to me," said Lady Ilarhia.

"I repeat, you are mistaken, there is no one else here."

Hieronymus edged closer to the door and peeked out. Lady Ilarhia sat imperiously on her mount, radiating cool anger at Monszer standing resolute before her. Reynald was close behind, keeping watch and fingering his sword menacingly. Of Derrend, there was no sign.

"I weary of this. Derrend!"

A terrified Kuulman marched into view with Derrend behind. One fist twisted the boy's robe while the other held a blade tightly against his neck. Hieronymus could see a thin trickle of blood seeping down Kuulman's quivering throat and the smirking visage of Derrend behind.

"Stop!" The Monszer patted the air nervously before him. "Let's talk about this. You don't need to threaten the boy."

Hieronymus felt nauseous. *How had it come to this?*

"I'm done talking, Monszer. Give me the other one now."

The Monszer appeared shaken by the violence so casually offered by the Lady Ilarhia and her companions. His gaze wandered between her and the young Kuulman in apparent confusion. Hieronymus watched him wrestle with the dilemma, to give up one unknown boy in trade for the life of another that shared his beliefs and devotion.

Monszer shoulders slumped in defeat.

Hieronymus had brought this danger to the priory. If he had not become enthralled by the lessons, the books, the kindness of the people here and simply moved on this would not be happening. Hieronymus reached a decision and his fear drained away. Everything was clear now.

"Derrend!"

Derrend grinned maniacally.

Hieronymus stepped into the courtyard. "Stop!"

"No." The Monszer moved to intercept him.

Hieronymus waved him away. "It's the only way."

"No, you don't understand." Monszer blocked his path, his expressive eyes held firm resolve. For a second they were the only two people in the courtyard, and Hieronymus sensed Monszer was trying to tell him something, something important, but Hieronymus was too emotionally bound in his decision to understand. He stepped around Monszer and faced the Huntress.

Lady Ilarhia smiled triumphantly. She jerked a chin at Derrend. Derrend shoved Kuulman roughly aside while Reynald slid from his horse.

"Now Guri!"

A dull chunk sound and a thick bolt protruded from Reynald's chest. As he collapsed the Monszer burst into motion striking Derrend with feet and hands, the movements so fast Hieronymus could hardy see them. A series of facial strikes drove Derrend back, stunned and disoriented. Derrend's sword fell free after one hard strike to his arm, immediately followed by a sweeping kick that spilled him to the stones. Before he could defend himself, another blow struck the man unconscious. The Monszer turned to Lady Ilarhia.

The Huntress backed away, her eyes ablaze. She raised a clawed hand and spoke a word. The Monszer pitched over screaming. Hieronymus was caught in the spell. His entire body was afire although no flames were visible. He screamed and heard it echoed by others nearby. He rolled frantically trying to smother the pain; his chest aching as he strove to draw in desperately needed air. When an inhalation came it filled his lungs with racking heat that forced him into a coughing fit. He rolled on the stone, every movement agony to his seared skin, fighting for one more breath. He wondered if he was dying.

In the center of his agony was an oasis of respite, the memory of his near constant headaches, familiar and almost comforting in his torment, a tiny hole of lesser anguish in the firestorm. He embraced it as a sun scorched and thirsty man would a drop of water. He dove into his memory of relief and the burning disappeared. He stopped screaming and gasped in relief. The terrible searing of his being was gone.

He forced his eyes open, afraid of seeing the black and burnt remnants of his hands, his skin split and bleeding over cooked muscle.

Nothing! His hands and arms were unharmed. Hieronymus stared in bewilderment, his senses reeling from the pain he knew he had experienced to the reality of what he saw. *How was that possible?*

The Huntress was a sorcerer. It was the only answer. She had used her magic when Reynald and Derrend failed. She was still concentrating; hand flung out, gaze intense and severe, while a drop of sweat trickled down her brow.

Hieronymus was terrified and awed at the power she wielded. No wonder sorcerers were hunted and killed. To fell all four of them with a word was frightening. It was also dangerous, to have that much power. The screams around him were weakening, interrupting his thoughts. He must do something; he must stop her before she killed his new friends. But what could he do?

Wait! He held that power as well.

Hieronymus concentrated on the oasis within him. He did not know what he was doing, but the waters expanded through his body, around him, dowsing the last vestiges of heat and cradling him in placid coolness. Slowly the pool began to swirl around, ripples spreading across its surface as it gained speed and merged with the pounding in his head, moving faster and faster until it was a maelstrom threatening to roil him in a flood of torrential power.

Lady Ilarhia must have realized he was not screaming like the others and shifted her attention. For a second, fear flashed across her face.

"No!"

He released the flood.

Ilarhia screamed as it knocked her off her mount, sending her rolling away like a tattered cloth in a strong wind. When she finally stopped, she lay unmoving in the dirt road outside the priory wall. Hieronymus stared wordlessly at what he had done. *What had he done?*

He shivered in the silence as a bone deep chill enveloped him in an icy shroud. When the chill passed, he weakly rolled onto his side and in confusion looked at the results of the deadly confrontation.

The Monszer staggered to his feet, ashen faced, a thin stream of blood leaking down his chin. Guri appeared and rushed over to Kuulman who lay there breathing laboriously. Lady Ilarhia's henchmen did not move. One had an arrow jutting from his chest, the other appeared unconscious or dead.

Hieronymus collapsed backward into the courtyard and stare at the sky. *Aellissea* still shown brightly but her heat failed to thaw the chill he felt. He shivered in relief and watched the clouds drift by as sedately as his muddled thoughts.

His former life was no more. He could never return to Braewickinn village. There was no longer any doubt.

He was a sorcerer, and a dead man.

"What will happen to me now?"

Monszer did not answer. They were once more in the sitting room, facing each other, yet neither seemed able to start.

"What do you want to happen?"

"I don't know," said Hieronymus. He jumped up and began pacing. "I didn't ask for this, this power, this curse. All it's done is cause trouble. It got me kidnapped, my best friend killed, and now I'm on the run from someone I don't even know. Someone who wants to kill me." He collapsed back into a chair, breathing hard.

"Who wants to kill you?" Monszer asked.

"Nimbus! Haven't you heard a word I said?"

"I heard. What makes you think they want you dead?"

"Because of what I am, a sorcerer." Hieronymus started pacing again. "I've heard the stories. I know what happens to magus once they're discovered. I, I don't want to end like that."

"Sit down, Hieronymus," said Monszer. "Let me explain some things to you." Once Hieronymus was seated, the Monszer began pacing.

"What you say was true, once. After the Great Burning, the people were afraid of sorcerers, with good reason. They were hunted, killed, almost eradicated out of fear of what might happen if their power got out of control. But some survived the purge. They remained hidden, or protected by those who control their power for their own purposes. Magical power is a rare ability these days. Those who control it are always on the lookout for more. That's why they hunt for magus, to retain and extend their sphere of power. They are not killed, just controlled."

"What?"

"Have you ever heard of Savant Baishur?"

Hieronymus shook his head.

"The Savant is a sorcerer. He works for the Emperor himself."

"But, I thought…"

"So, Nimbus isn't trying to kill me?"

"Probably not. Most likely he planned to sell you off to some ruler to become their personal savant." Monszer grimaced. "It happens. Especially when one is untrained."

"What should I do?"

"I have some ideas…"

The next morning Hieronymus went to speak with Lady Ilarhia.

Bruised and battered from Hieronymus' magical assault the monks had gagged and locked her far from everyone. It was an isolated guest room decorated in a baroque style more suited to the past century. Derrend was trussed up in the stables and Reynald buried near in the cemetery behind the keep.

Kuulman untied her hands and then stepped away, leaving her legs still bound and his gaze never wavering. At a gesture, she carefully removed her gag and worked the stiffness from her mouth as she watched Hieronymus closely.

Hieronymus was irritated. She acted as if everything was normal, even though she was the one locked away. He blurted out, "Why me?"

"You're strong," she said.

"What…"

"Nimbus likes strong," said Lady Ilarhia. She turned a pleading gaze upon Hieronymus. "Come with me. We'll both be rewarded if you come willingly."

"Go with you?" Hieronymus gaped at her gall. She wanted him to go with her now, after everything she had done to him. "Are you mad?"

"Nimbus will have you. He knows of you now. He won't stop until he has you. You're a fool to resist."

Hieronymus' clenched hands into fists while his head throbbed in angry heartbeats. She had kidnapped him, hunted him, caused the death of his best friend, and tried to kill Monszer and others at the priory. His tamped down anger broke, "No!"

The carved table splintered into pieces with a force that knocked Lady Ilarhia backward. Hieronymus felt an eruption of air pass over him like a wave but leaving him unaffected. Around him, carved statues and vases slammed against the walls. The massive four posted bed and bureau shifted positions noisily as they slid across the stone floor, while the heavy curtains tore away from the room's single narrow window. In seconds, the guest room looked like vandals had sacked it.

Hieronymus stood panting, breath visible in the still air, shocked at the destruction around him.

To his left, young Kuulman crouched with a protecting arm across his face, eyes darting between the damage and Hieronymus. Lady Ilarhia huddled tightly against the back wall, trembling visibly as she too gazed fearfully at Hieronymus.

He turned and left the room.

"Thank you," said Hieronymus, "but I can't stay."

He stood in the courtyard dressed for travel. His clothes were clean and patched, while a canvas traveling cloak rested on his shoulders, a gift from the Monszer. Guri approached leading Hieronymus' horse, now loaded with supplies.

"We'll hold them a week or so," said Monszer. "Plenty of time for you to disappear."

"They're dangerous," said Hieronymus.

"Won't get the chance," said Guri.

"Guri knows herbs," said Monszer. He slapped Guri on the shoulder. "We'll feed them something to make them sleepy and when they awake, they'll be far away and no danger to anyone."

Hieronymus looked around the tiny courtyard and the surrounding buildings, his home for the last month. The gardens were doing well. He could see fresh sprouts shooting upward almost visibly in the warming weather. His look skipped over the fresh grave where Reynald was buried, a painful reminder of their confrontation days before.

He breathed deeply. He had to ask. "What about Nimbus?"

The Monszer paused. Finally, reluctantly, he said, "Stay away from them, they're dangerous."

"But why?"

"I can't tell you. I know only hearsay and rumor and you need facts."

"Is there anyone?"

"Maybe," said Monszer. "There are brothers in Kyr-Darst who may know the answers you seek. Find our retreat there, and *Mrynlinn* willing, you'll get some answers."

Hieronymus mounted his horse, nodded goodbye, and rode away, his tall form looking ungainly atop the animal. The three followers of *Mrynlinn* watched Hieronymus until he rode out of sight.

"You could have told him," said Guri.

"It's not time."

"Makes no sense to me," Guri muttered.

"Nor I, wiser heads than ours made the decision."

Kuulman interjected. "You think its him."

"Only *Mrynlinn* knows."

Prince of Mules

Foreword

One of the curses of having an overactive imagination is that ideas come from everywhere and nowhere. One morning I awoke with another full-blown story idea that wouldn't let go. I decided to write the basics down and go back to a more pressing project. Wrote the core idea down, then added some of the cultural and societal ramifications, then had an idea for who the main character might be, and before I could stop I started writing the story itself. By that afternoon I was pushing 1400+ words and didn't want to stop. I didn't, and the following story is the result.

At first, I imagined the events were occurring in another fantasy realm and not part of Bulinnärm. That saddened me. I hate to waste ideas, so I thought about it some more as I gazed at the world map hanging above my writing desk. I had the entire Ulax continent completely empty of content and realized I had plenty of room to place some very isolated kingdoms and societies. A few map additions, some name changes to better fit my concept of the region and I had an entirely new Bulinnärm story for my canon.

As a final thought, I'm considering expanding the core idea into a series of novellas. I'm pretty sure there's a great story to tell here and one day maybe I will. In preparation for that day I've written my notes down and stored them away.

I hope you enjoy reading it.

"I don't feel so well," Prince Ruele mumbled.

"Let me see," the mule Ishaan said.

He touched Ruele's forehead with the back of a soft cool hand.

"You are a little warm." Ishaan frowned. "Nothing to worry about I think. Let's get you into bed and I'll grab something for you to drink. How does that sound?"

"Wine, could I have some wine?"

Prince Ruele, the eldest of nine siblings, let himself be led to a bedroom and tucked into a huge bed the Zsara mother said he'd soon grow up and into. Ishaan made sure he was comfortable before drawing the shades. He stopped to whisper with Tomin, Ruele's personal guard, and their identical brands and worrisome gazes sent a small shiver down his slender frame.

It took a long time for Ishaan to return and when he did, it was behind a crowd led by the tottering Zsara Nasriim, his pregnant mother. Her expression radiating calmness and control and one he had grown used to seeing over the years, but now he saw worry lines around her eyes and the slight downturn of her lips. She strode right up to his bed, her cerulean silk robe trailing behind like water, her ears and fingers bearing numerous gold ornaments with jeweled settings of jade and sapphire. Behind her, a constant gaggle of richly clothed advisors, leather-clad guards, and waiting servants hung back a couple of paces, providing the illusion of privacy where none existed.

"Ruele, Ishaan tells me you aren't feeling well."

"Yes mother," Ruele said.

"Not to worry, everything will be well."

Ruele recognized the empty promise in her words, it was something she said whenever she knew the truth might be too painful for him to hear. She had always protected him, sometimes to extremes. His coming down with this sickness was different, but he didn't know why.

She brushed his bangs away with one henna decorated hand and gazed tenderly at him from within more swirling designs.

"This is normal, everyone gets sick eventually, and now it's your turn." She patted a cheek. "Ishaan will keep an eye on you. Let him know if you feel worse as he knows what to do. And if he tells you to do something, its for your own good. Do you understand?"

"Yes mother, but–"

"No buts just do it. He speaks for me on this." She drew him close and hugged him briefly. Ruele could barely breathe in her fierce embrace, and then she released him and stood.

"The Viceroy of Ardashar awaits, your Majesty," said an advisor.

Zsara Nasriim Johhar, ruler of the Kingdom of Tagoore, gave Ruele a wistful smile and then strode out, taking the crowd with her. The sudden emptiness a vast relief for those left behind. As Tomin shut the oak door, Ishaan poured juice and handed it to Ruele.

"What did my mother mean when she said it was my turn?"

"Don't fret about it my Prince, drink up."

"But I want to know, why is it my turn?" Ruele looked over at Tomin. "You'll tell me, right Tomin?"

The big guard blanched behind his unruly graying beard and mustache while his eyes darted everywhere but where Ruele lay. When he did speak, it was blunt and final. "Not my place, my Prince."

Tomin was a man of few words and if he wouldn't speak then – Ruele had a terrible thought. He grabbed Ishaan's forearm and begged. "Are my brothers and sisters okay? They aren't sick too, are they?"

"No, no, the young zsarens and zsareens are fine. No need to worry about them."

Ruele let himself be soothed. As long as his siblings weren't sick then everything would probably end well. Soon the cool dimness and comfortable bed drew him into a restless sleep.

In it he dreamed he was walking along a road, a road unfamiliar to him and yet he knew it was where he was supposed to be. He was surrounded on both sides by wheat fields, tall and golden under the sun, with dozens of farmers harvesting the wheat for eventual sale to the market. One of them looked up to stare at Ruele. He looked exactly like Ishaan, his personal servant, the same sandy hair, same soft features, and same forehead brand.

The first Ishaan shouted and the other figures stood and looked as well. Suddenly, Ruele was afraid. They all looked like Ishaan! In unison the Ishaan farmers began walking forward, their eyes locked on Ruele, they're faces stoic and frightening. Ruele glanced behind him to see more Ishaan's approaching. He wanted to run but saw no escape as they came closer, closer...

"Wake up," said an urgent voice. It was followed by a sharp poke to his ribs.

"Ouch!" Ruele said sitting up.

His friend Jani sat grinning and munching on a heel of bread. Ruele's stomach growled. A tray bearing the remaining bread, a hunk cheese, a covered plate, and a pitcher sat on the dressing table next to his bed. It looked good, but it was too hot to eat just now. Maybe Jani would open a window for some cool air. He lay back and just looked at his friend.

Jani was older by a season but of such a slight build, many considered him younger. His hair was longer too, normally short and in constant disarray, it now fell below his ears and over mischievous brown eyes. As always, he wore a lopsided grin that never seemed to waver. When it was obvious, Jani wasn't going to speak first, Ruele asked, "What time is it?"

"Almost second watch," Jani said. He took another bite and spoke as he chewed. "I was thinking you'd sleep all night."

"I'm sick, you probably shouldn't be here. You might catch it."

Jani laughed. "I can't catch what you got, not me."

"You don't know that." Ruele was angry now. Jani wasn't listening at all.

"It's the change," Jani declared.

"The change? I've heard of it, but I've no idea what it is, or means."

Jani fell back, kicking legs in the air and laughing hard. When finished he shook his head. "It's a miserable time is what it is. You're growing into an adult is all? Soon your voice will deepen, you'll be noticing girls, and do more sword fighting than climbing trees or exploring. As prince, they'll give you duties that can't be shirked. No more playing, no lazier days running, swimming, and having fun. No more time for me."

Jani held up a hand before Ruele could protest.

"But worst of all, you'll get sick, like now. Everyone does, it can't be helped. When it passes they'll have to judge you."

"Judge me? What for? What's that even mean? I'm sick and they're going to judge me for that?"

"Oh, judging's important, very important, it sets you for life."

"My life is already set."

"No, listen," Jani leaned forward and whispered, "They judge whether you be a man or mule."

Pieces fell into place. Ruele knew mules, mules were everywhere in the palace, as guards, servants, they were the cooks, the stablemen, the gardeners. Ishaan was a mule, Tomin as well; in fact, everyone he knew in the palace was a mule with the exception of his father, Zsar Dhevranvanu Johhar. Mules did all the work, all the fighting, provided the craftsmen that made the goods and services mule merchants bought and sold. Mules were always men and wore a brand on their forehead that marked them so. But the one thing mules couldn't do was father a child, that was a breeder's job.

"I'm a prince, surely they'll judge me a man."

Jani shrugged. "From what I know, status don't matter, wealth don't matter, you're a mule until they examine you and say otherwise."

"That..that sounds barbaric."

Jani shrugged. "It's how it is."

A murmur of voices outside the door startled them. The latch began lifting.

"Bye." Jani scampered away leaving Ruele confused and alone.

Jani's information made his head throb in discomfort. The door began opening and Ruele pretended sleep as Tomin peeked in. Moments later Ishaan slipped into the room and replaced the tray Jani had foraged on with a fresh one.

"He's eaten a little," Ishaan said.

"Good, the lad needed it."

Both men gazed down with concern.

"What are the odds?" Tomin asked.

"He comes from a strong line, maybe three in five," Ishaan whispered back.

"That's all?" Tomin sounded surprised. "Put me down for twenty iron then."

"That's a lot, you sure you can afford it?"

Tomin glanced at the prince. "He's a good lad, he'll pass."

Ishaan shook his head. "That's nonsense, the judges don't care about his royal bloodline, just if he can breed. No breeding and he's out."

"The Zsara won't allow that."

"She won't have a choice. It's the law. Royal mules must be banished for the kingdoms own good."

"Bah, stupid law," Tomin said.

"Mayhap," Ishaan said. "I don't wish ill on the lad, but what choice do any of us have?"

The two men slipped out as quietly as they had entered.

It took a long time for Ruele to fall asleep.

The next three days was a nightmare of alternating fevers and icy tremors that constantly wracked Ruele's body from one extreme to the other. Like a ship caught in a storm, he fought to survive the burning thirst and damp sweaty sheets as the fever burned through his body. He could keep nothing down and slowly lost the energy to resist. When not burning up he was trapped by chills that no amount of warmth could alleviate. He shivered so hard he was convinced his teeth might shatter despite the mounds of pre-warmed quilts and oven hot bricks that surrounded him. When he was between bouts of fever or chills Ishaan was there urging him to drink or eat, but even the few bites he attempted refused to stay down.

Eventually he entered a dreamlike state of existence where nothing was quite real to him. People visited all the time. Ishaan was always around and sometimes his mother, the Zsara was there too, pregnant with another sibling, looking worried and demanding someone, anyone relieve his torment. Visions of Tomin lifting him and anxious servants replacing linens, and once Jani was there, a look of concern on his sympathetic features as he concentrated on helping Ruele drink.

On the fourth day his fever broke.

That afternoon he received a summons for judgment. It was on delicate parchment and penned beautifully, but the words were stilted, concise, and without nuance. He was ordered to appear for judgment in the Royal Hall in two days. Failure to appear would force them to issue a warrant for his arrest and subsequent execution.

Ruele realized how difficult it was to recover with a death sentence over one's head. Although he was starving, he barely managed a mouthful for the rest of the day. He tossed and turned all night but when breakfast arrived, he managed to choke it down and even asked for more.

"You feel up for a walk?" Ishaan asked.

Ruele nodded. He was tired of the sick smell in his room, even though servants had replaced all the linens and blankets with clean ones just that morning. His legs were weak when he sat up but the more he moved the better he felt. By the time Ishaan had helped him dress he was feeling stronger. Tomin had watched the whole endeavor without comment.

"Remember, take your time, you're still fever weak." Ishaan then spoke to Tomin. "To the market and back should be enough. Keep an eye on him."

The big man nodded. "Of course."

The day was perfect for a walk, sunny without being too hot, with a slight breeze blowing the salty smell of ocean up from the harbor. Ruele was glad to be out of the castle and moving, away from that sickbed for a time, even if he was moving a little slowly and accompanied by a guard.

Ruele's imagination had been working overtime since his fever broke. He had so many questions and Jani knew only a bit more than he did. All his life he'd accepted the social order of mules and breeders but somehow he never made the connection on how it might affect him. Now it was a question of vital importance. He looked up at the armored man next to him. Tomin had been his personal bodyguard since birth and Ruele trusted him with his life. He was also a mule, and if anyone would know, it was Tomin.

"Tomin, what's it like, being a mule?"

The big man looked down with a wry smile. "Wondered how long it'd take. We're not even at market yet." His steps took on a looser, almost staggering walk. "Best thing in the world to my mind," Tomin said. "Your kind of free, not tied down like breeders. And women, plenty of them only want some fun and mules can provide that."

Ruele face frowned. "Fun? Like dances and parties?"

"You're a bit young to understand, but something like that." Tomin continued walking and Ruele followed along. The market was thriving today as they passed stalls loaded with produce and grains, clothing and jewelry vendors, while snake charmers and mystics demonstrated their skills. "Don't get me wrong, breeders can have fun as well, but then they marry off and the first wife takes control. After that, it's whatever the first wife wants, he ain't got much say."

"He don't?"

"Naw, first wives are responsible to the family, in making it grow and prosper. She finds other woman to bring into the family, and the man breeds them all. The more males they produce, the better their chances of creating a new breeder. That brings them more status with other families, and power as well. It's how the Johhars, your family, got to be rulers of the kingdom, by breeding true and gaining status."

Ruele spotted a farmer selling cherries, a popular fruit that grew easily in the kingdom and one of his favorites. He dragged Tomin over to the stall. "Can we get some?"

"Can't hurt, but don't eat too many." He handed Ruele a handful of the luscious fruits and stowed the rest in his pouch. They began retracing their steps. "Ishaan will cuss me out if you don't eat dinner."

"What about mules? What do they do?"

"Pretty much everything else. We're everywhere doing the chores, making barrels, shoeing horses, milling grain to flour, trading, guarding. You name it, we do it."

Ruele ate the last of the cherries and discreetly wiped juicy fingers dry on his britches. "Doesn't sound too bad to me."

"Well, that's cause you're not seeing it all. Take me; I don't mind being a mule. Never wanted a family, or living with a single woman my whole life. But others, well, they burn for them things, a family, children, a wife and home to call their own. Its something they can never have, and that makes them sad and even bitter. It's a sorry thing when a man can't pursue that what the common animals enjoy, makes a man the lesser for it."

The gate guards passed them through the castle gate without challenge. Tomin rubbed the raised scar of his mule brand.

"Course, this branding hurt like hell, but it fades after a time." He placed a comforting hand on Ruele's shoulder. "I believe you'll make your mum proud, and tomorrow night you'll be wondering what all the fuss was about."

Ruele's forehead burned in sympathy as he tried not to think about tomorrow.

The judgment hall was the largest room in the castle. Ruele was familiar with the room as it was often used for ceremonial events, state dinners, dancing and holiday balls, as well as public trials and meetings. The stately walls rose high overhead where sunlight illuminated noble banners hanging from aged beams and filled the room with light and soft shadows.

Today the chamber was setup as a court, with three raised chairs on a raised platform at one end and rows of benches facing them for observers to sit. Every seat was packed with townspeople with more standing in the back. Palace guards with phlegmatic expressions kept watch over the attendees as people talked, bickered, and argued good naturally with their neighbors and friends. It was an exciting day for them and most planned to enjoy it as best they could.

Ruele peered nervously at the crowd. "Why are all these people here?"

"To see you lad." Tomin laid a comforting hand on him. "Not everyday the commons get to see royalty judged. It's a big day, a very big day."

Standing in line before him were four more youths awaiting judgment and a senior guardsman. All wore their best holiday clothes for the ceremony with the guardsmen in his best armor. He didn't know any by name but knew their families lived and worked in the palace. All looked as scared and sick as he felt.

There was a blare of horns and the banging of metal on stone as the chamberlain's staff struck the floor for attention. His stentorian voice echoed off the walls. "All rise to welcome Zsara Nasriim Johhar, Queen Ruler of Tagoore and all its lands from the Serpent Ocean to the Bluewood."

The crowd grew silent and stood as the Zsara's expectant figure entered from a door on the far wall, followed by her attendants. Ruele spotted his father, the Zsar of Tagoore, among them. He looked far older than his mother and moved as if he too was recovering from sickness. The szara and her entourage settled into waiting chairs, followed by the rest of the room. His mother looked as she always did, calm, in control, and showing not a bit of concern about the upcoming ceremony.

More figures exited the door and the chamberlain continued. "The court includes Justice Avapooriun, senior scholar Chuubri testing, and General Sanu, chief defender of Tagoore, witnessing." Ruele swallowed as the three men lined up before the assembly wearing identically grim yet dignified expressions.

The chamberlain's staff banged the floor again.

"All present shall bear witness to this judgment. Share this with those unfortunates who could not attend, spreading the honesty and truth of Tagoore law to all its citizens so that they too can know the decisions made today by these worthy subjects."

The chamberlain stepped back and Justice Avapooriun stepped forward, an ascetic looking man with gaunt bony features under a saffron turban and matching robe. "Your majesty," he said and bowed. Behind him, the scholar and general did likewise. Zsara Nasriim dipped her head in acknowledgement and the men straightened.

"Have those summoned to this judgment arrived?"

"They are," the senior guardsman said and marched into the chamber. Behind him trailed the four boys and Ruele, with Tomin bringing up the rear.

Ruele instantly felt every eye was on him. His entire focus was concentrated on the boy in front of him and taking one slow step after another while trying not to panic. People in front murmured to each other as he passed but he couldn't understand a word over the pounding of blood through his ears. It took forever to reach the chairs placed before the wooden barrier and then turn to face the judges. He waited nervously with the other five boys.

Justice Avapooriun spread his hands and began. "People of Tagoore, we have before us five brave candidates who wish to join our kingdom as citizens and practice our cultural heritage. Most will become productive citizens of the kingdom, free to take up any trade or service as they desire including the defense of our wonderful kingdom." One hand gestured at the nearest guardsmen. "A few will have an equally important role, that of breeding the next generation so that we can survive as a kingdom." This time the hand gestured at Ruele's father sitting with the Queen. "Both tasks are vitally necessary and important. There is no shame associated with either class, both are critical to Tagoore's strength and wellbeing. No, there is only duty, duty to themselves, duty to our Queen, and duty to the kingdom of Tagoore."

"We judge these boys today to determine their future duty to all of us. To do that we offer proof of our methods. Scholar Chuudri, if you would."

"Thank you, Justice Avapooriun," Chuudri the scholar said with a smile. "I hold here the sacred rod of *Murjainen*, the God of Justice, and it will choose each boys duty. Allow me to demonstrate."

General Sanu joined the scholar, as did a young woman bearing a shallow bowl. The general held a large knife that he raised for all to see.

"My name is Nagisuchi Chuudri and my duty to Tagoore is as a breeder. I bear no brand, and offer my 28 children as proof and have sworn statements from my wives of their husbandry. My blood is the blood of a breeder. General, if you please."

The scholar held out his empty hand and in one quick motion, the general sliced the palm open. Blood dripped freely into the waiting bowl until the scholar squeezed a fist halting its flow. The girl turned so all could see the blood.

"The judgment."

Chuudri touched the tip of *Murjainen's* rod to the blood.

Ruele jumped as a flash of green smoke erupted from the bowl and the crowd cried out. The grassy smoke drifted upward to dissipate in the rafters overhead. The girl displayed the now empty bowl for all to see.

"Green is the color of a breeder, an indication of growth and harmony for all." He turned to General Sanu. "General."

The general was a mass of hard muscle and grim visage. His voice was rumbling deep and reverberated around the chamber. "I am General Indrepel Sanu, commander of Tagoore's army. My duty to Tagoore is to protect it from our enemies, and I do that as a mule." He touched the brand on his forehead. "I bear the brand proudly and my blood is the blood of a mule."

Without hesitation, he swiped the knife across his palm and bled into the bowl. The girl displayed it again but when scholar Chuudri touched the blood, it burst into brown smoke. Even braced in anticipation, Ruele flinched when the blood changed.

"Brown is the color of mules, indicating a protective nature, a trader's spirit, and a closeness with the kingdom," Chuudri proclaimed.

Justice Avapooriun spoke. "Thank you, fellow judges. Its time to begin judging."

A new guard appeared from somewhere and escorted the first boy to stand before the judges. The girl held out the bowl, the general sliced, and blood flowed. After a moment, the cut was bound and everyone waited for the test.

"What is you name?"

"Hasa Dasahim, your lordship."

Scholar Chuudri touched the blood and a whoosh of brown smoke roiled upward. "Let the kingdom know that Hasa Dasahim is judged a mule from this day forward." Ruele heard a cheer from the crowd, possibly the boys family, while the guard escorted him away.

The second boy was brought forward and tested. His blood transformed into another cloud of brown. The third fainted when the smoke erupted in green to great cheers and shouts from the crowd. Ruele started to worry. If Ishaan was right, only one boy in five was destined to breeder status. His parent's bloodline was strong in producing breeders, but was it strong enough?

Ruele nearly fainted when the fourth boy's blood burst into green smoke as well. The crowd's cheers and celebrations went on for a long time. Two breeders from the same judgment, an auspicious day indeed. Ruele wanted to vomit, his stomach rolling as he realized the chances of being declared a mule was now a certainty.

"Relax lad, everything will be fine," Tomin whispered.

Ruele could barely walk forward when gestured to do so, Tomin by his side. It seemed the crowd had become unnaturally silent as he approached the judges. All he could hear was the lub-dub, swishing sound of his own heartbeat as he crossed the marble floor.

The three judges loomed over him with cold, stoic expressions The girl held out the shallow azure bowl and he reluctantly placed his hand over it. She winked at him as he did. He was so surprised he never felt the knife cut cleanly across his open palm or his lifeblood dribble out.

This time Justice Avapooriun spoke. "What is your name?"

"Ruele Johhar, your judgeship."

Scholar Chuudri leaned forward and touched the blood. There was a flash of light and then a curl of white smoke that smelled of burning copper and seethed into the air like an escaped beast. Scholar Chuudri fell awkwardly, as Justice Avapooriun and General Sanu reeled in surprise. A woman screamed, and then pandemonium took the crowd. Angry shouts and curses filled the chamber.

"Tomin, what –"

"Monster!" Someone shouted.

A man crawled over the barrier and raced towards Ruele. Tomin knocked him down. More were clambering over as the man hit the ground.

"Come on," Tomin said. He began dragging Ruele from the chamber.

He heard wails from the galley and saw his mother slide off her chair in a faint and attendants swarming to help. Ruele tried to pull loose, to run to her but Tomin's grip never lessened as they exited the chamber. The last thing Ruele saw was Ishaan's frightening dead stare.

Ruele slumped in a sitting chair contemplating his cut and bloody palm. It had finally stopped bleeding, but now it hurt something awful.

What does it mean, the white smoke? They hadn't declared him a breeder or a mule, so what was he? Where did he fit? And why had the crowd turned into an angry mob? He didn't know and no one would answer his questions. Tomin had rushed him away and locked him in his room before disappearing. Ruele raged against the door, kicking and demanding, then weeping and begging someone to tell him what was going on? After a while he gave up and fell sulking into a chair.

Now in his exhaustion all he felt was shame. Shame at his non-status, shame at himself for still acting like a child when he should be an adult, a man, despite not being a breeder or a mule. He was of royal birth and that meant assuming greater responsibility. So far, he'd shown none of that.

He heard a noise and Jani walked in from another room. Had Jani been waiting in there all this time? His friend rushed over and pulled him out of the chair.

"Why are you still here? You've got to run. Now!" Jani tugged his arm, nearly dragging him. Ruele pulled free, he was done with others leading him around. He was of noble birth; he would stand and act on his own from now on.

"I'm not going anywhere, not until I get answers."

Jani glanced fearfully at the door and then back. "You really don't know?"

"Know what?" Ruele spread his arms in exasperation. "I'm locked in here. How would I know anything?"

Jani touched his arm gently. "Ruele, they want to kill you."

"What?"

"The white smoke, people are saying it's a curse. If the Queen wasn't in labor right now—"

Panic surged through him. His mother was in labor. He had to go to her, see her, let her know he wasn't responsible for the white smoke. He turned to rush the locked door and demand his freedom when Jani grabbed him.

"Stop that, stop." Jani was restraining him. "They won't let you near the Queen now? They won't even let you out."

Ruele slumped in defeat. His friend was right. Tomin had locked him inside alone and then abandoned him just when he needed someone to talk to. Where was everyone? His mother was busy giving birth but where was Ishaan? Shouldn't he be here? He closed his eyes and tried to think. Who could he talk to? Jani?

Ruele opened his eyes. "Is she all right?"

"She was, last I knew." Jani patted a shoulder. "She's done this several times before, I think she'll be fine."

"But, what about Tomin? Ishaan? Where are they?"

"I don't know," Jani admitted. "It doesn't matter. You can't be here when they do arrive."

"But why? You're not making any sense. Why should I run? I haven't done anything wrong. Once my mother hears of this, she'll make it right. She's the Queen, she can fix it?"

"I don't think so. People were frightened by your judgment. The judges were arguing its true meaning when I left."

"You were there? I didn't see you."

Jani looked away. "Well, I was. After you left the Queen was rushed away and the guards forced everyone out. They were saying terrible things about you, and the Queen, about demons and curses and purging the evil. That's why I ran here as fast as I could. You need to get away, give them time to calm down."

"I won't run," Ruele said. "It will shame the family."

"You'll be dead if you don't."

"But they'll call me a coward."

"A live coward is better than a dead prince, at least in my book."

Jani cocked his head and put a finger to lips. Outside the door they heard the clink of weapons and armor just before someone knocked. It was loud, slow, and rattled the door in its hinges.

"Prince Ruele," Ishaan said, "Unlock this door. I have important news for you."

"Come on. Its time to go."

"But it's Ishaan, I know him." Ruele protested.

"Prince Ruele, I know you're in there. Open this door now."

"Not anymore," Jani said grabbing his arm. "Come on."

Jani led him into his study room, where tutor after tutor had spent countless hours instructing him on everything he needed to know to be a prince of Tagoore. Taking his hand Jani led him into a closet and shut them inside.

The sound of axes pounded at his bedroom door.

"We can't hide here," Ruele hissed. "They'll find us."

"Ssshh, just shut it." Jani was fumbling around one wall. Ruele heard a click and a portion of the closet wall slid aside. Jani pointed into the dark recess. "Go, climb down."

A crackle of splintering wood sounded outside. Muffled shouts followed. Ruele fumbled until his hand found a slat on the far wall. His foot followed and then he was descending, one slow step after another. Dust rose and filled his nostrils in the cramped space as he made his way down. Above him, Jani appeared and closed the hidden door. Darkness swallowed them and it became even harder to take each step, his reaching foot fumbling for purchase.

The descent went on forever in Ruele's mind until his foot met a hidden floor. He slid sideways to make room for Jani. His eyes were adjusting and he could just see his friend peering up the hidden ladder.

"Come on."

Jani took his hand again and proceeded to get him lost in a maze of dark passages, sudden turns, and ladders leading both up and down. It felt like forever and he was sweating and suppressing coughs in the stale air between the palace walls. Jani moved through the maze of passages with an ease Ruele could only admire. Why had his friend kept this wonderful secret from him? They could have had great fun over the years eluding his many keepers.

Finally, they stopped and Jani flipped open a tiny eyehole and peered through it. Satisfied, he opened the wall and stepped inside. Ruele followed and almost immediately backed out again, blushing furiously. It was a wardrobe, filled with the fragrance and clothing of a young woman's belongings. Jani grabbed his arm and pulled him back inside, then shut the door.

"We can't stay here. It's improper."

"Pipe down," Jani said. "You're safe here. Who'd expect a prince to hide in a girl's closet? No one."

"Who's is it?" Alarm sounded in his head. His eyes darted away from a pile of semi-transparent shifts. "It's not my sisters room is it? Tell me these aren't Raatma's clothes."

"Ouch!" He rubbed his shoulder where Jani had struck him. It hurt. "What was that for?"

"To shut you up," Jani replied. "Settle down, I use this place all the time, its safe. The owner has others they use more often. Besides, it has something you need."

Ruele kept trying to find someplace his eyes could rest without actually looking. He settled on Jani's face. "What do I need?"

"Clothes."

"I'm not wearing any of those."

Jani swept several delicate robes off a battered chest and began scrounging around inside. Before long, he tossed Ruele some clothes. "Put those on."

The clothes were dull brown, stiff, and of heavy cotton, made for durability, not fashion. So different from the fine linens, silks, and satins he normally wore.

"I can't wear these," he protested.

"You'll be captured within the day wearing those," Jani said. He gestured at Ruele's holiday clothes, an ocean green tunic that fell over black trousers to his knees, both detailed with fine stitching and pearl buttons. Jani pointed out. "Your only chance is to look like everyone else. Put those on."

Ruele grumbled but had to agree. He began undressing. Jani abruptly turned to the chest and burrowed more as Ruele changed. His friend muffled voice continued.

"We'll get you a horse. I have the perfect one for you. She's very sweet and a good runner. You should head north first, towards Ardashar, or that's what you want people to think. Once you can't see the city and no ones around, head east into the woods until you reach the river. Find the river trail, you'll know it when you see it, and follow it until you can cross over and continue east. Here, you'll need these too." He tossed Ruele a floppy hat with a wide brim and a faded green cloak that had seen better days.

Ruele remembered the river trail. He and Jani had once explored it on horseback without attendants or permission and been gone nearly a full day before Tomin and the other searchers caught up with them. It had been a wonderful day of freedom.

"The Gap first and then Kist They're your only choices." He waved a hand. "Turn around."

"What?"

"I've got to change too."

"Oh, right." Ruele turned away, trying not to stare too obviously at the delicate garments before him as his friend changed.

He heard a deep breath. "Okay, I'm ready."

Ruele turned and stared. A nervous looking young woman in simple cottons like his stood where Jani had been. She was petite, with shoulder length hair, large mischievous eyes, Jani's crooked grin, and a worried expression.

"Jani?"

She winked at him and Ruele recognized her as the young woman with the bowl at his judgment.

"That was you?"

She nodded. "Suunjani, Jani to my friends."

"But you, you're a girl."

"I wanted to tell you, but I didn't have the courage." She looked down. "Now you're leaving and I can't do this anymore."

"But why did you hide? I don't care."

"But others do." Suunjani's large brown eyes implored him to understand. "Girls and boys can't mingle except under supervision, and I hated everything they wanted me to learn as a girl. Sewing, dancing, poetry! I wanted to explore the woods, swim, ride horses, do exciting boy things."

"So I changed clothes, changed my name, and met you as Jani. I never thought you'd see me like this, ever."

Ruele was reeling. His best friend was a girl. He shook himself. No wonder he'd never spotted Jani at the palace, hidden within a crowd of girls. His sisters probably knew her, but he wasn't allowed to mingle with them except under supervised activities that involved the entire palace.

"But we've no time. Do you have any money?" Before Ruele could shake his head, she handed him a money purse. "Hide that, you'll need it later."

Suunjani packed his old clothes in the chest as he stuffed the purse inside his trousers. Slamming the lid down she buried it under several garments and began securing her hair underneath her own wide-brimmed hat.

Ruele fingered the hidden money purse inside his borrowed clothes. "You were planning on running away, weren't you? All of this, these clothes were for you. Now you're giving it to me. Why?"

For a long time Suunjani remained silent, arms clasp tight around her in reassurance. Finally, she turned to him and there were tears on her cheeks.

"You don't know what it's like here. You think you do, but you're a boy, almost a man now. It's different for girls. The lucky ones marry at our families order or a first wife's whim to become brood mares for enhancing the family status and size. Those not chosen as wives might as well be mules for all the consideration they get. Sure, we can dally with mules, they have the equipment, but we can never have a family of our own, children not destined for a prearranged life."

She brushed the tears away. "I wanted more. Have you ever read *A Thousand Tales of Skar*?"

Ruele grinned. "Of course, I love that book. Ishaan read those stories to me when I was a child. I wanted adventures like Skar. I mean, who didn't."

"Well, I loved them too. I was always in trouble for reading them. Those are for boys, my tutors explained and took my copy away. I wanted to be Skar, just like you. So I became Jani instead and started having my own adventures."

"I remember now, you were always looking for trouble." Ruele grinned at the memories. "But somehow I was the one that got blamed."

Suunjani grinned. "You are pretty slow at times."

"Am not."

"Are"

They laughed and suddenly it didn't matter to Ruele that his best friend was a girl. He and Jani had done their best to have adventures within the confines of the palace and sometimes outside as well. When the laughter faded away, they looked at each other in silence.

Suunjani opened the hidden door. "Come on, let's find you a horse."

Once again, Ruele became lost in the hidden passages within the palace. Suunjani led him quickly through the dim and stuffy passages until they emerged inside a storage room filled with barrels and sacks of flour and grains so tightly packed they had to squeeze between them to get out.

Suunjani led him to the stables along a circuitous path he'd never seen before. From a distance they were two youngsters at play and ignored by the few adults they saw.

"Where is everyone?" Ruele asked.

Suunjani shrugged. Her eyes were in constant motion and wary. "Who cares, makes it easier for us. Here we are."

Ruele kept the cloaks hood up as Suunjani led him to the stables. Inside, she led him to a stall containing a placid gray mare that looked at them with a solemn eye before going back to chewing. Suunjani made baby sounds as she stroked the mares neck and haunches. The mare flicked her tail in response.

"She doesn't look like much, but old Rhoohanna is the best horse here."

Suunjani led the horse to the stable door by a rope halter. She nuzzled the horse's nose and cooed at her with affection. Between affectionate pats and strokes she continued with instructions.

"You'll need to ride bareback so as not to attract attention. Stay off the main roads, and avoid people. Once you get to the river, abandon her and walk. She'll find her own way back." Suunjani patted the mares nose gently.

Ruele had an inspiration. He didn't have to do this alone. He gripped her arm. "Come with me. They'll be looking for a boy, not a boy and a girl. We'll fool them and get away."

Suunjani pulled away. "No, just save yourself, please?"

Disheartened, Ruele climbed onto Rhoohanna's broad back while gripping her mane in a close grip. He was familiar with riding and normally enjoyed the experience but not without tack and saddle. That might take getting used to. As if sensing his nervousness, the mare glanced back in reassurance before placidly returned to eating.

He looked down at Suunjani.

Ruele thought about how she had given up her dream of escape to help him. She was gazing fearfully back into the stables. His friend, for she was still that despite the years of pretending, was forsaking her dream to help him. How could he thank her? He didn't have a clue.

There was movement in the stable's door and Suunjani was urging him on. "Go, don't run, trot."

Ruele urged Rhoohanna into motion. He concentrated on staying on the horse's back as they trotted away. He glanced behind him as a knot of guards entered the paddock. His last view was Suunjani's terrified expression before being surrounded by guardsmen.

Ashamed for abandoning her, he urged the horse on.

The rest of the day was uneventful. Rhoohanna led him along trails as if born to them, avoiding the main trade roads whenever possible. Ruele kept a constant lookout for any followers but saw nothing. The few peasant farmers he saw were too busy working their fields to point at them and cry 'the prince' as he passed.

In all Suunjani's planning, she had forgotten one important item, food. Ruele's stomach growled harder as the day wore on. He'd hardly eaten anything for breakfast and nothing since. And he was thirsty as well. It was a mild day but the continuous riding motion and nervous fear worked together to parch him as never before.

The sun was going down when they finally reached the river. Ruele nearly threw himself onto the bank to drink from its cool waters. Rhoohanna did likewise, spreading her forelegs wide as she drank. When both were satisfied, Ruele led the horse along the bank. He was searching for a means to cross but in the fading light, nothing was obvious.

He thought about Suunjani's instructions. Should he release Rhoohanna now? He found himself reluctant to do so. She had unerringly led him to his destination and the next stage of his journey, but she was also a link to his past, a connection to Suunjani.

He shook his head in amusement. All those years and he'd never guessed his best friend was a girl. What else had he missed? What did the white smoke of his blood mean? Was he doomed to run forever?

He came upon a small copse of trees near the river, loamed with soft earth and grasses. Despite his hunger, Ruele was weary from the day's events. He pegged Rhoohanna where she could satisfy her hunger on the abundant grass and petted her softly.

"Rest well tonight," he whispered. "I'll send you home tomorrow."

Then he found a soft area in the lee of a tree trunk, settled his cloak around him and was asleep immediately.

Tomin was crouching nearby when Ruele awoke, looking tired and drawn. Ruele scrambled to his feet and backed away. How had Tomin found him? His head darted back and forth but saw no one else. What was Tomin doing here? Dare he run? No, Rhoohanna was placidly cropping dew dampened grass but Tomin would be on him before he could reach the horse.

Backing away, Ruele said, "I'm not going back. I can't go back."

The guardsman continued chewing a grass blade. He waited in the stoic manner all guardsmen eventually adopted when spending endless hours on guard. Patient, unperturbed, implacable as stone.

Ruele grabbed a fallen branch and waved it wildly before him. He knew he didn't stand a chance against the larger, more experienced man, but he wasn't a child anymore. He'd resist as best he could, all the way back to Tagoore if necessary.

"They want to kill me," Ruele said. "They came to my room, broke in. Why would they want to kill me? Why Tomin?"

Tomin watched him silently without expression. Tomin wasn't normally a quiet man. He'd been more than a bodyguard as Ruele grew up, an advisor, almost an elder brother at times, good natured, open, and friendly as a man could be with a youngster. But not this silent knot before him.

"Say something," Ruele commanded. He gripped the branch tighter and whipped it through the air in a menacing manner. "I won't go easy. I'll fight you, all the way."

Tomin spat out the grass stem.

"Well, you found me. What are you waiting for? Do your duty."

"I am my prince."

Ruele blinked. What did he mean?

Tomin was suddenly closer. Ruele swung the branch but the larger man tore it away and tossed it aside. Ruele tried to run but a strong hand held him firmly in place. He fought, but it was like a kitten fighting a bear hound. In seconds he was sitting down, breathing hard, with newly bruised knuckles. He stifled his resentment at the former bodyguards manhandling.

"I'm not going back."

Tomin stepped back and crouched down so their eyes were level.

Ruele couldn't meet the man's gaze. "I'm not," Ruele repeated.

Tomin nodded. "Then what are your plans?"

Plans? What was he going to do? It had all sounded so easy when Suunjani explained it, run away from the kingdom's guard, hide in some faraway town and forget his former life. Never see anyone he knew again. Not his mother, his father, or Suunjani.

But that brought up other problems. What was he? He wasn't a mule or a breeder, so what exactly was he? Would they let him escape? What if his enemies didn't stop searching for him? Would he ever be safe? And who were they?

It came out as a whisper. "What am I?"

"A prince of Tagoore, that's what you are."

Ruele slumped. A prince on the run, that's what he was, until they took his birthright away and declared him an enemy of the kingdom. What would happen then?

"The white smoke, what was it?"

Tomin shook his head. "I've no idea, and from the general commotion, no one else did either."

"Then why is someone trying to kill me?"

The big guard shrugged. "Don't matter, they'll have to go through me first." He gripped Ruele's shoulder firmly. "I'm sorry I left you alone. I shouldn't have. When I found the door broken I knew I'd let you down, let my honor down."

Ruele recognized the guard's expression, fear mixed with a crushing sense of failure. Tomin had been afraid, for him. Relief flooded through his body, draining away his own resentment and fear.

Ruele clasp Tomin's arm. "You didn't know?"

The guard shook his head. "No, my prince, if I'd suspected…"

Ruele threw himself into the bodyguard's arms with abandon. Startled, Tomin was slow to react but when he did Ruele found it hard to breathe. He gasp out. "You'd have probably died."

"True," the bodyguard sighed.

They stayed that way as tensions faded and Ruele's belly growled. Sniffling, Ruele pushed himself away.

"You wouldn't have some food, would you?"

Tomin handed him the butt end of a bread loaf. It was dry and a day old but to Ruele it tasted wonderful. He gnawed until there was nothing left.

"What are your plans?" Tomin asked.

"I don't know," Ruele said. Should he continue to follow Suunjani's plan? It wasn't very good but he had nothing better, but maybe Tomin did. "What would you do, Tomin? If you were me?"

"Me? I don't know. Run I guess."

"Run?" Ruele gaped, he had never imagined Tomin running from anything.

"Well, if someone's trying to kill me and I can't fight back, the only choice left is running." He smiled crookedly through his graying beard. "Can't fight if you're dead. So you wait, prepare, and go after them when they least expect you."

"But why? You escaped, right?"

Tomin pierced him with a hard eye. "You can't leave enemies behind boy. A dead enemy is the best enemy. They can't come after you then. Best to finish them off and be done."

Ruele considered the bodyguards advice. It made sense in a practical way. Since the ceremony he had become a danger to some faction within the kingdom. He didn't understand how or why, but the presence of white smoke had created enemies, enemies that wanted him dead or worse. He shuddered at the latter.

Worst of all, he had no idea who they were, or why they considered him a threat. All he knew was that someone was after him, and but for the help of Suunjani, he'd be in their hands even now. His surprise escape had certainly not been imagined by his enemies. It had surprised him, but he sensed they wouldn't stop searching until they found him. He had to run away, far away, and hide, hide better than he ever had in the palace. Then he could seek an explanation, try to learn why they wanted him so bad.

But where?

"We have to run," Ruele said. He faced Tomin nervously. "And we have to hide. Any suggestions?"

Tomin shook his head. "Jani said you was heading for the Gap. Makes as much sense as anywhere."

The Gap was a good start. "We're going through the Gap, maybe all the way to Kist."

"Never been to Kist," Tomin said. "I hear the women are divine."

Ruele laughed weakly at Tomin's single mindedness. Who said you couldn't take the mule out of Tagoore? "We'll get there, maybe one day."

He wished Suunjani could join them as well. No, he dismissed the thought. It was too dangerous for her. This wasn't a Skar adventure, it was real, and the consequences unknown and possibly deadly. He stood and slapped the dust from his britches. Tomin cocked his head.

"Come on," Ruele said. "We've got answers to find."

The Missing Wizard

Foreword

This is a short story I wrote after completing the initial draft of An Empire Forgotten, book one of my fantasy trilogy. I woke up one morning with the entire concept in my head and spent the day writing a first draft, some 3400+ words. It also involved my first female lead, the intriguing Master Librarian Alethea Vincencé. She appears in my fantasy novel and points an older Hieronymus onto the next stage of his journey. She becomes much more important in the sequel if current plotting holds true.

It has the distinction of being the first short story I'd ever seriously tried to write and self-publish as an ebook. I've since discovered that I have a tendency to write long. My short story plots don't get really exciting until about 4000 words into them, the time most short stories should be ending. I must admit though, I do like writing verbose and envy writers of tight stories.

The messenger pouch was waiting on her desk when Master Librarian Alethea Vincencé came into the sunny room that served as her office. Unlike the letters and other daily correspondence that arrived every morning, a pouch communiqué was not an everyday event. Her heart beat a little faster as she considered what waited inside.

Did it hold the answers she sought?

She brushed back an auburn curl that had come loose as she took a slow deep breath. If the message contained good news, then she could enjoy it with a good cup of kaffe. If the news was bad, she'd need the bitter drink to provide her some energy. Either way, kaffe would be important.

She glided over to her chair as a small speckled cat watched her intently from its perch on a sunlit window ledge, nestled between two plants bursting with colorful flowers. She ignored the cat's inspection, carefully avoiding all eye contact. She'd learned from experience that any attempt to recognize the feline would be construed as unwelcome and a rapid exit would soon follow. Why the cat continued to come back was the real mystery. It only tolerated her, but adored Hieronymus.

Alethea frowned as thoughts of the missing wizard intruded.

Hieronymus had the opposite effect on the cat. He claimed to have an affinity with animals. Whatever he had, the gray feline couldn't get enough of him. When he was around it followed him around like a dog, often curling asleep on his lap or shoulders as he translated tomes for hours. All that came to an end when he disappeared.

She sat down and sighed. *Where was he? And why had he left?*

Alethea chanced a look at the reclining feline. It sat between the plants with eyes half-closed, dozing softly in the morning sun. Maybe it missed him. Maybe she did too.

A side door opened and her assistant Gilly came in carrying a tray with the morning infusion of kaffe, fresh picked fruit, and warm rolls from the kitchen. It smelled wonderful. Gilly placed the tray on the desk and began pouring.

"Good morning, ma'am," said her assistant with a plump dimpled smile.

Gilly was an older woman that had served on the library staff for decades. Alethea knew she had a son and a daughter living in Choy, her husband a handler at the stables. Her long relationship with the library staff was one of the reasons Alethea had chosen her for the position, her gossip kept Alethea informed on the true state of the library.

"Morning, Gilly," Alethea replied. She peered hungrily at the morning's offering and selected an item. She took a delicious bite. "Strawberries are ripening."

"Yes, ma'am. Cook says the pickings are good, so you'll see a lot of them in meals over the next few weeks."

"I'm not complaining; tell her they taste wonderful."

"Yes, ma'am. I will." Gilly moved over to the window plants to check them for dehydration. The cat ignored her assistant completely, to Alethea's annoyance. If she had tried to check the plants the cat would have bolted like its life was in danger.

"How's Anna getting on?" Alethea asked. She sipped at the kaffe, then added two drops of honey. Ah, perfect.

"Oh, you know cook." Gilly returned to the desk and crossed her arms across an ample bosom. "Fruits are coming in nicely, but the butcher can't seem to fill his orders lately. Cook's so mad she wants to spit the man in place of the missing shanks."

"She wouldn't," Alethea laughed, "would she?" Alethea made a mental note to have the butcher questioned. Keeping her scholars happy and the library running smoothly was essential, and being short of meat at mealtimes would cause no end of complaints.

"Of course not, but she might beat him with a ladle he comes up short again."

"Good, thank her for the lovely breakfast, and you for toting it here."

Gilly inclined slightly at the compliment. "I will, ma'am. Will there be anything else?"

"No, I don't think so." Alethea glanced at the courier pouch.

Gilly smiled. "Some answers, ma'am?"

"Maybe, we'll know soon."

Gilly bowed and departed, leaving Alethea alone with her kaffe, the courier pouch, and a lightly snoring cat. She sipped again at the kaffe, reveling in the stillness of the morning. She nibbled at the breakfast Gilly had left until she couldn't eat any more. She refilled her cup with kaffe and felt ready to start.

Alethea picked up the courier pouch, noting that the Alexiandrölarn seal was unbroken. With trembling fingers, she broke the seal and pulled out the folded parchments inside. Nervously she spread them on the desk and began to read.

Library of Choy
Master Librarian's Office

My Dear Alethea,

It was wonderful to hear from you after so long. How many years has it been? Too many, I'm sure. We really should plan a meeting the next time either of us are travelling. Unfortunately, I don't see any travel in my future, but if you should ever return to Alexiandrölarn, there is a wonderful place of dining I just know you'd love. It offers the most succulent dishes. Don't keep me waiting.

As to the matter in which you inquired, I am sorry to say that I have nothing to report. My many inquiries have fallen on deaf ears and lax record keeping. Astounding what goes on without a strong hand at the tiller, but I'm afraid our current headmaster is not bestowed with much governance. He is, instead, over burdened with the sense of his own importance and not one to let daily routines interfere with his pursuit of external importance.

I made some additional investigations and have had no more luck then the official ones.

No one remembers, nor is there any record of a scholar named Hieronymus having ever worked within this university. From your description, tall, rangy, loud, and a bit cantankerous, you'd think it would be easy to find someone who remembers a figure like that, but alas, that has not proven to be the case.

As to his having worked for the Savant Bashuir, may he rest with the goddess, once again I can find no record or memory of such a relationship. In the final years of his life the Savant did have a research assistant, called Churanjeevi, a small nut brown man of quiet demeanor and voice. I am told he returned to Kist shortly after the Savant passed and that no one has heard from him since. I have sent letters of inquiry to friends within the Royal Academy there as to this assistant and I hope to hear from them soon on this matter.

One final puzzling item that my mind kept returning to while I was gathering this information.

The Savant returned to the Goddess in his 93rd year, after decades of service to the court of Alexiandrölarn. He had an entire cadre of assistants, the

*most senior of which was this man Churanjeevi, a well liked man by all
accounts, but he was in his mid to late 60's when he left the court to return back
to the Empire. The remaining assistants were younger, but would have been of
the most senior ranks for one of the Savant's status, placing them in their 30's
or 40's at least. And since the Savant passed some 40 years ago that would
make most of them old men as well. If the age of this Hieronymus is mid-50's,
then he would have only been a child during the final years of the Savants life.*

*I am sorry I do not have better news for you, but I fear you've been taken
in by a charlatan, one that means you no good. Should you have any more
dealings with this scoundrel, I would urge that you report him to the authorities
of Choy for investigation.*

Sincerely,

Your friend and humble servant,
Olice de Trevelliun
Scholar Emeritus of Alexiandrölarn University

Alethea dropped the letter to her desk and sat back, her lips pursed in
thought. That certainly made things clearer.

So, no one named Hieronymus ever worked for the Savant Bashuir. Did
he think she wouldn't check?

It seemed that Hieronymus was not entirely truthful with her. She
snorted, then looked around to see if anyone had heard. The cat had one eye
open and an expression that said, "Why are you disturbing me," before closing
it again.

If he had not been in Alexiandrölarn working for Savant Bashuir, where
had he been? And he knew about the Savant's albinism, not a common fact at
all. With that one fact his story rang true, and now she knew it for a lie. Maybe
he knew someone close to the Savant, maybe this Churanjeevi had told him.

She'd accepted his story, like a gullible child.

But why lie to her?

The ancient tome, *The Nature of All Things Living* was why Hieronymus approached her. There was something in there, or something he suspected was in there, that he wanted to find. What could it be? She'd continued translating the tome after he'd disappeared and found nothing unusual. There was still more to translate but so far, nothing but Orcalle stories, birth and death records, and some monologues on nature.

Was she missing something?

Alethea wracked her brain looking for something she may have overlooked. Hieronymus just appeared one day demanding access to the tome. The fact that he could read it a minor miracle. If the scribe Taolin hadn't brought Hieronymus to her they may never have met.

Wait!

Hieronymus hadn't come straight to her at all. Scribe Taolin had extracted a bribe from the tall wizard, and when he'd returned days later to check on it, forced himself into her audience. Her reply? She'd sent a note to him the same day. His request, where was it?

Alethea ransacked her desk seeking Hieronymus's request. Eventually she found it tucked between an odd order for cold weather cloaks and her evaluation of Scholar Bealdwine's latest dwarfish trade route report.

The Fire Monkey Inn, what an unusual name. That's where he'd wanted the reply sent. Maybe someone there could answer her questions about him? Only one way to find out.

"Gilly, I need my cloak!"

Alethea stepped from the tunnel entrance separating the Inner City from the sunlit streets of Choy. She raised her face towards the sunshine and reveled in its warmth. She had not set foot outside the shadow of the *evest* trees of the Inner City for weeks and welcomed its shiny glory.

One of the young guards manning the tunnel smiled at her shyly. "Ma'am, do you want someone to accompany you?"

Alethea smiled back, bringing a blush to the man's face. Noting the brightly shined hound insignia on the collar of his spotless jacket, indicating a new officer, she replied. "Thank you, okezar, I'll walk alone today."

"It's no trouble, ma'am."

Alethea stopped. "Oh, there is one thing you could do for me."

"Yes ma'am."

"Could you have one of your men talk to the library's cook. A butcher is shorting her orders. I'd like to know why."

"Yes ma'am, I'll have someone look into it today." He bowed his head in acknowledgement. "Will there be anything else, ma'am?"

"No, I think that sufficient, don't you?" Alethea waved goodbye over her shoulder as she strode lightly away.

It was a gorgeous day.

Alethea made her way south following one of the main roads that bisected Choy, making it easy to get anywhere with ease. The Seaway road was one of the main routes between the docks to the North and the desert caravans to the South, and crowded with merchants carting trade goods in both directions. She fell into line behind a chain of local porters carrying huge bundles on their heads. She wondered what the bundles contained. Rolls of cloth from Strothkurn, woven rugs from Irlum, wines from the vineyards of Brularn? Trying to guess made the walk pass rapidly, and before she knew it they arrived at the Southern staging area, the gathering place for merchandise heading to Gulgash or the dwarven kingdom of Dugalduruun.

Breaking away from the line of porters she started searching for the Fire Monkey Inn. An older woman selling veils pointed her in the correct direction.

"Ye can't miss it, My Lady. Oh, this color would look wonderful on you."

Before long she stood outside her goal, a two story building huddled between two others of more ramshackle appearance.

The sign carried a crude but colorful drawing of a monkey juggling three flaming coconuts. Alethea shook her head at the sight, *How strange.* With firm steps she mounted the stairs and entered the wide doorway.

Inside, the cool interior of the inn's common room was a welcome relief from the rising temperatures outside.

A woman appeared from the back toweling her hands dry.

"Welcome, can I help you?"

Alethea glanced around nervously. Now that she was here, she had no plan on how to continue. The woman stood patiently, waiting for her.

"I'm not sure." She smiled shyly. "I was hoping to speak with someone, someone that could help me."

"What kind of help are you looking for?"

"It concerns an acquaintance, a friend maybe. He's missing, and I'd like to find him."

"Does this friend have a name?"

"Hieronymus?" Alethea held her hand well above her head, "Very tall, a bit arrogant, and a wizard."

"Hieronymus?" The innkeeper sniffed loudly. "What's that fool of a man done now?"

"So, you know him?"

"Know him, I'll say. Come, sit yourself down. I'll grab something for us to drink."

"If you're busy…"

"No, no, I'm glad you came by. Might make that husband of mine appreciate me more when he returns." The woman pointed her to a booth and departed. Alethea removed her cloak, sat and jiggled her leg absently as she looked around.

The room itself was small, but well proportioned and comfortable at first glance. She was impressed by the shiny brass lanterns hanging from every other column, the large fireplace that covered the far wall, and the well used but cared for tables and chairs arranged neatly in the middle of the room. Along the walls were snug booths where a pair of customers sat, one eating from a generous tray of food, the other hunched over and sipping quietly from a large tankard.

The woman returned in moments bearing a tray with two glasses, a wine bottle, and a small plate of cheese, bread, and fruit.

"Oh my, that looks wonderful."

"Thank you. It's not often a fine lady comes to the Monkey. Especially one that knows Hieronymus." The woman's eyes twinkled with suppressed mirth. "My names Saara by the way. Keke and I own the Fire Monkey. It ain't much, but it's ours."

Alethea waited for the wave of words to pass. Feeling slightly overwhelmed, she replied. "I'm Alethea, I'm, I mean, I work at the Library of Choy."

Saara swept her extremely long black hair out of her face as she poured a light colored wine into the glasses and slid one over. Up close, Alethea could see Saara was only a couple of years younger than herself, with perfect bronze skin and a bright smile. Alethea flicked some imaginary dirt off her skirt, uneasy with the relaxed, cordial demeanor of the other woman.

"A learned lady, I can see why Hieronymus likes you."

Alethea felt a flush in her cheeks. So Hieronymus liked her? She filed that away for later examination. They had gotten along quite well she had to admit. Right now though she needed information that would help her find him.

She took a small sip of wine that tasted remarkably good. "We were working together and he disappeared. I was hoping to learn why."

"Ah, so he left you did he?"

"Yes, no, I don't know." How did this woman manage to cut right to the core of her concern? It was uncanny. Alethea plucked up a piece of fruit and took a bite, chewing slowly while mulling over the woman's words.

"Excuse me for a moment," said Saara.

The innkeeper got up, thanking the eating customer as he left the inn, then retrieved a fresh tankard for the other. The heavily built man barely acknowledged the refill, returning to his drinking with determination. Saara cleared the other table and then returned.

"I'm sorry," she said softly, "I can be a bit forward sometimes. I didn't mean to make you uncomfortable."

"No, no, that's all right. It was, was most refreshing actually."

To Alethea's surprise, she meant it. She had few friends at the library, both from her position and the fact that most of her associates were male. The few woman scholars were a lot like the male ones, singular in purpose and driven to uncover as much knowledge as possible, and none of them pursued a course that would place them in a leadership position, like her.

"You were asking about Hieronymus."

"Yes, it's been more than a month since he disappeared. I kept thinking he'd be back soon, but now I'm really worried. He didn't strike me as someone who leaves things undone."

Saara nodded her head in agreement. "No, he isn't. That man has always been too curious for his own good." Through pursed her lips she choose her next words carefully. "He got himself into some trouble and had to leave town."

"He left town?"

Saara patted the back of her hand in sympathy. "Yes, I'm sorry to have to tell you this. He got into some trouble gambling and left with a young man named Archer. They joined a caravan heading south, to Gulgash I think."

"He left for Gulgash? With Archer?"

"Yes, I'm afraid so."

"Well that's a relief." Alethea felt a great weight disperse. Relief that Hieronymus was still alive, followed by anger at his callous treatment toward her. How dare he leave without telling her? All those courtesies and polite conversations didn't mean a thing to him. He'd been manipulating her the whole time.

Something in her expression made Saara sit up straight and point a finger at her. "You're the Master Librarian, aren't you?"

Alethea briefly considered denying it, but the woman was being open with her, it was only right she do the same. "Yes, I am."

"Well, don't that beat all. He may be a fool, but he does have good taste in women. I'll give him that." The innkeeper refilled the glasses.

"Hieronymus didn't strike me as a talker. Did he talk about me?"

"Oh no, like a clam that man." Saara worked to suppress a smile. "No, it's what he didn't say. If you catch my drift."

Alethea did, and she could feel a flush rising in her cheeks. She quickly took another sip of wine to recover her poise.

"At least I can stop worrying."

"Oh, you can't do that. Men like their women to be worrying. Makes them feel wanted I think." The two shared a sisterly glance and knowing smiles. "What more can I tell you?"

"Well, anything I guess. You say he left with Archer? Why was that?"

"Well, after cheating the biggest casino in town out of a lot of money, he and Archer got into a fight with some casino thugs wanting their money back. They managed to kill all five of them and came here."

Alethea felt the blood draining away, "He killed five men?"

"They'd have killed him if he hadn't. Archer helped, so he didn't kill them all."

"Were either of them hurt?"

"Archer was cut up a bit, nothing serious. Anyway, I fixed them up and Keke introduced them to a caravan leader. The next morning they were gone."

Alethea considered this new information. A message from Gulgash would take a month to get back, assuming the miscreant remembered to send one. She sighed in resignation. If he came back, she'd deal with him then. In the meantime, she still had a manuscript to translate.

"If you hear from him, would you let me know?"

"Of course."

The other customer chose that moment to noisily depart the inn. A huge man, he had trouble navigating around the furniture between him and the door. Saara and Alethea did their best to ignore his stumbling departure, then broke into laughter when he was gone.

"Men," they said in unison, laughing.

Alethea donned her cloak. "Thank you for speaking with me, and for the delicious food and wine. I feel so much better."

Saara offered her hands and Alethea clasp them warmly. "I enjoyed meeting you, Master Librarian. Please come again."

"Alethea, please call me Alethea."

"Okay, Alethea, please come again. I enjoyed our conversation."

"I will, Saara. I will."

Alethea started to depart, then turned back. "I must ask, where did you get the name Fire Monkey?"

"Oh," Saara said with a blush.

"Never mind, I think I can guess." The two shared another laugh and Alethea took her leave, her spirit lifted from learning about the wizards absence.

The late afternoon crowds were lighter in the heat of the afternoon, many taking the opportunity to sit in the shaded groves scattered throughout the city. Alethea considered which route to take back to the library. Determined to get an answer to Hieronymus's absence that morning she had hurried, but now that she knew, a more leisurely walk back through some of the public gardens sounded in order. Yes, that was a good idea. While she spent most of her time in the gardens of the Inner City, the public gardens held their own unique interests.

Her mind made up, a large shadow engulfed her in masculine scent, a large arm wrapped itself around her while a hand covered her mouth. Stunned at the sudden attack, she was carried into an alley where she began struggling helplessly.

Her attacker ignored her wriggling and continued walking. Unable to struggle free, Alethea bit and tore at the soft flesh covering her mouth. There was a gasp of pain and the man dropped her in a tangle onto the ground.

Alethea recognized her abductor, the drinking man that had stumbled out of the Fire Monkey. Cursing, the man shook his hand in pain, ignoring the blood dripping into the dirt. He yanked Alethea to her feet with his good hand, then shook her until dizziness left her unsteady.

"Weren't no call for that."

Alethea swayed in his grip. "Let me go. I order you to release me."

"Now, now, you're not the one in charge here. Answer my questions and you can go." He leaned in close and Alethea noted the dark stubble on his heavy jowls. "I'm looking for that wizard, just like you. Tell me where to find him and we won't have to get intimate," he leered at Alethea with a broken smile, "if you know what I mean."

Alethea swayed back from the man's sour breath. She drew herself up straighter, trying to control the sudden fear that bubbled up inside. Had someone seen her abduction? Where were the city guards? Surely someone would help. "You were there. You must have heard as well as I. Now let me go."

Alethea tried to jerk her arm away but the man's grip didn't loosen.

Her abductor smirked, amused by her rebellion. He pulled her closer, until there bodies were nearly touching. Alethea tried to shy away but his grip never yielded.

"Not yet, tell me where he is."

"Gulgash, maybe Dugalduruun by now. I don't know where he is." She was pleading now, her voice quivering.

"Not good enough."

"I've told you. Please, that's all I know."

Alethea tried to push herself away. It was like pushing against a wall. Fear settled in her stomach, she was helpless. Oh, why hadn't she accepted that guards offer. Tears welled up in the corner of her eyes. "Please, let me go?"

"Where is he?" The man's grip on her arm tightened painfully.

Sudden anger burned away Alethea's fear. With a yowl, she turned to claw at the man's face and kicked towards his groin. The man grabbed her free arm and casually blocked her kick with his hip. She heaved and bucked trying to get free. It was no good.

"That's enough." The man hooked both her arms with one hand and slapped her again, harder. The blow disoriented her and once her vision cleared she found herself hanging from his grasp and tears streaming down burning cheeks.

"Please, please let me go."

"You need manners, bitch."

Alethea tried to avoid his swing, but was too slow. The fist drove directly into her middle, and suddenly she had no air, just an aching emptiness. She tried to draw a breath, but her stomach muscles were locked in rigid agony, refusing to release. She felt herself falling as she was released. Darkness edged her vision as she struggled for air even as she lay curled in the dirt.

A hand grabbed her hair and yanked her forcibly upright.

"My turn."

Alethea closed her eyes in resignation. She had done her best, but she had been no match for him.

"Hey!"

Alethea heard the yell as she struggled to breathe, barely aware when the big stranger was yanked away. Released, she curled tighter, a wounded animal struggling for air. Her clenched muscles finally relented and she drew in a single desperately sweet breathe, then another. Dimly she was aware of a fight going on nearby, the scuffling of feet, the grunting of effort, the thud of blows on flesh.

She forced her eyes open to see who her rescuer was.

Saara!

The innkeeper Saara stood oddly, her arms raised before her as if orating, but with cupped hands stiff fingers, reminding Alethea of a snake's head. Saara stood confidently poised on her feet, swaying back and forth slightly as one might when holding a small child. Her face serene, showing no trace of fear or anxiety, just fierce determination.

The big stranger growled, then moved on the small woman, trying to overwhelm her with swings of his massive arms. Saara swayed away from each blow, avoiding them effortlessly. Before each arm could withdraw, she struck them so rapidly that Alethea could hear and see their effects. Her attacker grunted in pain then backed away, shaking each arm stiffly.

Alethea drew herself up, looking around for anything she could use as a weapon. A board, a brick, a pebble.

Roaring in fury, the man charged the innkeeper, his arms outstretched, fingers curled and ready to grapple, where his superior strength and size would work to his advantage. His huge form enveloped the tiny form and Alethea feared for the woman.

"Saara!" Desperately she threw herself at the man's back, fearing the worst.

Even as she moved, the strangers head jerked back, twice, then Saara slipped away from the clasping arms with a move as elegant as a dance step. The move left her standing to her attackers exposed side. Without pausing she struck rapidly with her elbow and Alethea heard ribs crack. Saara continued her dance step rotation and kicked sideways at a bent knee. It broke with a sound that made Alethea wince. The man collapsed to the ground screaming.

Saara stepped back, her face composed and calm. Without another glance at her opponent she grabbed Alethea and led her into the Fire Monkey, through the common room and into the kitchen. By the time Alethea was sat down, she was crying and shaking badly. Someone handed her a towel and she buried herself in it, trying to hide her fear and shame.

It took a while before the shaking and crying drained away and Alethea felt her fear fading.

"Are you all right?" Saara handed her a glass of wine before sitting on the bench next to her. Alethea looked into the innkeeper's concerned expression as she took a sip. An Irlum vintage, not your typical serving wine.

Alethea offered a tiny smile. "I think so."

A large man with mahogany skin and the thick musculature of an islander stomped through the door. Alethea shied back but Saara stood and hugged the newcomer. Smiling, she said, "Alethea, this is my husband Keke. Keke, this is Alethea, the Master Librarian Hieronymus spoke of."

"Ma'am, it's an honor."

"No, the honor's mine. Sorry for disrupting your home."

"Don't worry about that, we'll be fine." Keke hugged Saara's shoulders and smiled. "Who was that man?"

Alethea's chest constricted at the memory. "I don't know. He wanted to know about Hieronymus. Where he was? But he wouldn't believe me when I told him I didn't know."

"Probably a thief looking to rob him." Keke clenched his jaw in anger. "I wish I was here when it happened."

"I do too, dear, but Alethea and I handled it."

Alethea thought Saara's explanation was a bit exaggerated. She had done nothing, it had been Saara all along. Alethea remembered Saara's strange dance steps that overwhelmed her attacker. She had never seen anything like it before.

"What was that?" Alethea asked Saara. "The fighting dance, I mean?"

Saara laughed. "It's called *jaroom-sinduu*. It's a form of islander hand fighting I learned as a girl."

"It was impressive, I'll say that."

"Would you like to learn?"

"Me? I don't know."

"Please, I insist. It'll give you a reason to visit and it'll help me stay in practice. Please, I'd love to share it with you." She glanced sideways at her husband. "Besides, Keke doesn't like losing. He's gotten a bit slow lately."

"Now wait a minute."

The women laughed.

A bit grumpily, Keke asked, "I'm told you were here about Hieronymus."

"Yes, I was."

"I don't know if I can tell you much more than Saara did. We spent a few years fighting together in the Thousand Kingdoms, but I can't say I know him well. He's a loner that comes and goes on his own schedule. Hell, I've known him for two decades and I don't understand him any better then the day I met him."

"Thank you. That actually helps a lot."

"What did I say?" Keke looked confused.

"You said he's your friend." Alethea held her hand out until Keke clasped it, then squeezed reassuringly. "And that's all I need to know. If you trust him, then I will too."

"Just like that?"

"Just like that." Alethea smiled and stood. "I really must get back. There's a tome that needs translating. Maybe it will tell me what he's looking for."

Against her protests, Keke accompanied Alethea safely to the Inner City tunnel. After a quick thanks she went directly to her rooms and a restless night of sleep.

The next morning Master Librarian Alethea entered her office, moving awkwardly after her encounter yesterday but with resolution. She was determined to channel her fears into something more useful. Maybe learning to defend herself would help.

She stopped, another courier pouch with the seal of Alexiandrölarn gleaming bright in the sunshine that fell across her desk. She approached slowly and sat. She didn't notice the pair of green feline eyes that tracked her movements from the window ledge.

Once again, fingers trembling, she broke the seal and read.

Library of Choy

Master Librarian's Office

My Dear Alethea,

I have received replies from my friends in the Royal Academy in Kist, but I think it is not the answer you are expecting.

No one in the Royal Academy has ever heard of the scholar called Churanjeevi. They were quite adamant about their information. While there have been some students with that name, it being rather common in the Empire, never has one obtained the rank of scholar nor travelled to this esteemed university to act as an assistant to Savant Bashuir.

This is most strange.

That the man you sought information about, Hieronymus, was never here, and now I discover that a man that was here for decades, Churanjeevi, never existed in his claimed homeland or attended this university.

I fear something is wrong with this history, with those men. But I know not what I should fear. Except for you. I fear for you now that I've told you what I've learned.

I beg you to avoid any contact with this man should he make himself known to you again. Contact the authorities immediately. I am concerned for your welfare even more than before. Be careful.

Sincerely,

Your friend and humble servant,

Olice de Trevelliun
Scholar Emeritus of Alexiandrölarn University

Alethea sat back, letting the parchment fall to the floor.

The man she knew as Hieronymus was somewhere to the south, far away from Choy, according to Saara.

But, who was Hieronymus?

# # #

A Post Introduction

In the summer of 1980 I was discharged from the Marine Corp and living with my mother in a manufactured home outside the little town of Gladwin, Michigan. The economy was rotten at that time and I didn't have my own car so getting anyplace was a major pain. One day we made the trek to Saginaw to shop at mall and that's where I found the most interesting game I'd ever encountered.

Actually, I wasn't looking for a new game, I was looking for new fantasy books to read, hopefully a series I could dig into over the long days of a Michigan summer. What I found dominated my thinking for decades in one form or another and is the reason you hold these stories now.

It was a hardcover book called the *Dungeon Master's Guide*.

Basically it was guide for creating fantasy setting in game form and contained a dictionary of terms, rules, charts, and other fascinating data a person could use to design and run their own Dungeon & Dragons campaign. I devoured it for the rest of the summer. Before I was finished reading I was already constructing dungeons and stories, all I needed were some willing friends.

I found some and over the summer we began playing. I documented everything as I had an inkling these memories might one day be useful. Once we stopped a game to go see a new movie that sounded pretty good. It was more than good and *Raiders of the Lost Ark* stoked our enthusiasm to play even more. For the next two years we played whenever we could and then I returned to the Marine Corps.

In 29 Palms I found a whole new set of interested players and we soon had a weekly campaign going with two of us acting as rotating DMs. Somewhere around this time I got serious and created a map of my new fantasy world, christened it Bulinnärm, and began systematically leading players into interesting areas for fun and adventure. That same hand-drawn and inked map hangs above my computer for easy reference to this day. Again, I made notes of my players adventures for later use.

When I was discharged for the second time I went into technical writing and over the next two decades worked for some of the most innovative companies in the world. I concentrated on the software side and had a successful career writing software manuals, creating instructional materials and training people, as well as managing teams of writers supporting dozens of products.

In 2000 I began toying with writing a fantasy novel. I had several exciting scenes in mind but no story to tie them together. I played around with several projects but none ever took off. Of course, I stored all of this design work away as well, for later.

In 2010 I came back more determined than ever to write fiction. I pulled out all the material I'd saved, reviewed it completely, and then figured out my story basics, the lead, the supporting characters, the general places they would visit, some of the trouble they would find themselves in, and other plot twists and fantastical images. I needed feedback, so I joined an online writing site and began churning out my first fantasy novel with the goal of posting one chapter a week. I learned a lot in that year of writing, most specifically how to write a 3500-word chapter a week that made sense, and when it was complete, I moved onto the second book of the trilogy.

What? All fantasies are trilogies, aren't they?

So things were looking good, and then I stalled, I blocked, and I gave up in disgust.

It just wasn't right. I'd read enough over the decades to know when a story works and when it doesn't, and while some of what I'd written was fine, other parts had to go. Trouble was, at that time I didn't know how to fix the problems. But I tried. I read writing books, rethought the plot, the characters, reworked scenes and – came up empty.

Then, one morning I awoke with an idea, a great idea.

If I couldn't work on my novel, why not write smaller stories?

So I did, and that day I wrote the first draft of *The Missing Wizard*, a kind of side story that explored a major character in a way she hadn't had a chance to develop in the novel.

So, now I go back and forth. The fantasy novel is still a work in progress, as is its sequel, and a couple other novels, and more short stories than you can shake a stick at. You can see a list of my current projects at my web site turovich.com.

This volume you hold in your hands via print or ebook is the result. A collection of short stories set in Bulinnärm that span the ages, explore various locations on the map, and introduce interesting people and events in my fantastical realm.

So, welcome to Bulinnärm. It's my world, and I want to share its stories with you.

I hope you enjoy them.

L Frank Turovich
October 2015, Austin, Texas

Afterward

If you enjoyed this book and want to read more, visit my website at turovich.com. There you'll find blog posts on my writing progress and other topics of interest to me and hopefully you. While you're there, add your email address to my Reading List to receive a personalized newsletter and I guarantee, no spam.

In addition, if you're really motivated, think about posting a review on what you've read wherever you purchased your copy. Reviews are extremely helpful to indie-publishers like myself in spreading the word that someone enjoys our stories. Honest reviews always help me find new authors to read and follow, so share your enjoyment with others.

Here's some additional sites where you can find me on the web:

Website: http://turovich.com

Amazon: http://amazon.com/author/lfrankturovich

Facebook: http://www.facebook.com/lfrank.turovich

Goodreads: http://www.goodreads.com/author/show/ 1618254.L_Frank_Turovich

Twitter: http://www.twitter.com/lfrankturovich

Other Stories

Short Stories

Adventure
Pirates of Misfortune
Carving Time

Science Fiction
Nemesis Probe
Saving Brackett Station

Young Hieronymus
The Huntress
A Lesson in Power
Amaranthine Dreams

Skar Doorishmurk
A Painful Blessing
An Angry Mountain (coming soon)

Bulinnärm
The Missing Wizard
Prince of Mules
Chronicles of Bulinnärm *(collected short stories)*